The Long Gray Target:

Book III

FANGS OF THE WOLF

By

Roger Maxim

This is a work of fiction.

All characters, except known historical figures, are imaginary and any resemblance to actual persons is coincidental.

Cover Art courtesy: "U-boot" Augusto Ferrer-Dalmu

OTHER TITLES BY
Roger Maxim

(Short Reads)

Aluminum Rain

Mosquito Bites

Legend of White 19

(Full-length Novels)

Red Flight, Break!

Pacific on Fire

The Long Gray Target
      Book I: Don't Shoot—I'm Neutral!
      Book II: Shadow On The Sea
      Book III: Fangs of the Wolf

Tuesday
December 8, 1942
Newport Naval Station

USS *Woodside* (DD-203) is a Clemson-class destroyer built in October, 1920. She is the classic "four-piper"—a ship having four smokestacks. Here she is, over 22 years old, still in active— VERY active—service. She was presently swinging at anchor at the Newport (Rhode Island) Naval Station, her usual home port.

Woodside had just returned from taking part in the Operation Torch landings in North Africa and, upon her return, had received bundles of mail. In that mail were official notices of promotion for some of her officers and men:

George Radcliff to LTJG (Operations Officer)
Jacob Woodman to LTJG (Administrative Officer)
Leonard Wirtz to Soundman 1st Class
Phil Summers to Radioman 1st Class
Peter Perkins to Radioman 3rd Class
Paul Kondorski to Machinist Mate 1st Class
Tony Lutier to Electricians Mate 2nd Class
Emil Paskowitz to Bosuns Mate 2nd Class

Woodside's Captain, Commander Edwin Palmer, was pleased that his men were successful and gaining in experience. The men happily left the ship for liberty ashore to celebrate their advancement with friends.

* * * * * * * *

Lieutenant Junior Grade George Radcliff was especially happy to return to Newport. He left the ship and quickly headed for the Naval War College that is located on the base. He entered the beautiful Luce Hall and headed for a corridor flanked by offices. He walked resolutely to almost the far end where he found Office 168. He entered and immediately smiled:

"Hello, Lucinda."

The young lady in question looked up sharply at the sound of his voice:

"George! Oh, my! What are you doing here?"

He grinned:

"We just got back yesterday and you are my very first stop. How are you?"

She laughed:

"How am I?" She glanced around the momentarily empty office to ensure that no one else was present: "I'll show you how I am!"

She jumped up, rushed to Radcliff, and wrapped him in a tight hug:

"Now that you're here, I'm fine!" She leaned up and kissed him firmly on the lips.

George couldn't smile because she had his mouth covered but when she backed off:

"Wow!" He exclaimed breathlessly: "Now THAT is what coming home is all about!"

He held her tightly, rejoicing in her closeness.

"Lucinda, is there any way you can get the rest of the day off? I'd love to spend the day—just the two of us!"

She grinned:

"Let's go ask Professor Stalling."

The Professor was happy to see Radcliff, too, although there were no hugs or kisses.

"Of course, Miss Wallings, please take the rest of the day off and welcome this sailor home from the sea!"

Lucinda and George did just that.

By late morning, the pair was walking happily, hand-in-hand, down the Thames Street sidewalk looking for somewhere to have lunch. Somewhere to eat—but also somewhere to get warm—the temperature was 36 degrees and the wind was blowing. Their hearts were warm but the rest of them was cold.

Coming up on the right was a place called "Sam's Restaurant". To George, the term "restaurant" seemed a bit grandiose, but he assumed they probably served food and the place was probably warm. They entered.

It was a bit close and fuggy, but that was a welcome relief from freezing. As they entered and got their bearings, George was surprised by a group of voices calling out:

"Hey! Look! It's Prof!" Another voice: "Hey, yeah! Hey, Prof!" Yet another: "It's Prof! ...and he's with a girl!"

George turned and saw several sailors in a booth about halfway along the right wall. They were familiar sailors.

Lucinda looked at him:

"George, do you know those men?"

"Yes," he smiled, "some of them are men I work with in the Ops Center."

"Why do they call you Prof?"

George thought about it, and then responded:

"Well, come here and I'll introduce you..."

As they approached, the fellows in the booth stood in respect for the young lady:

"Fellows, this is my"—he hesitated—"friend, Lucinda Wallings from the War College. These men are Leonard Wirtz, Joey Donatelli, Peter Perkins, and Mike Torelli.

Lucinda smiled:

"I'm pleased to meet you." Then her curiosity got the better of her: "May I ask you a question? Why do you call him 'Prof'?"

Joey smiled:

"Me, Peter, and Mike went through boot camp together with— Ensign—Radcliff. His college paperwork got lost, so he went through like an enlisted guy with us. After boot camp, they found the papers and he got to be an officer. But everyone in boot camp started calling him 'Prof' because he's really smart, and because he used to be a teacher."

Radcliff smiled as he asked:

"So what are you guys doing here?"

Joey grinned:

"Wirtz just got promoted to Soundman 1st Class and Perkins to Radioman 3rd Class. We're sort of celebrating."

Radcliff got a funny expression on his face. Joey noticed and asked:

"Uh, Prof, is there a problem?"

Radcliff smiled and shook his head:

"No, Joey, not a problem at. Congratulations Wirtz! Congratulations, Perkins! And…they're not the only promotions."

"Huh?"

Radcliff grinned:

"You are now speaking to Lieutenant Junior Grade George Radcliff of USS *Woodside.*"

Happy congratulations exploded from the men around the table and Radcliff was very pleased. He also enjoyed the proud gleam in Lucinda's eyes.

Wirtz spoke above the noise:

"Sir, would you folks join us here in our booth?"

Radcliff was fully aware that officers do not socialize with enlisted men, and Wirtz knew it, too. But this was different—they were friends from boot camp—boot camp—of all places!

Radcliff thought about it, but he realized the invitation was actually a compliment, so he glanced at Lucinda who nodded imperceptively.

It was a happy group who stayed well into the afternoon sharing stories and laughs.

*   *   *   *   *   *   *   *

In an office at the Naval Station, Commander Palmer was engaged in a conversation also:

"Well, Stu, as the Officer in Charge of destroyers, what exciting new news do you have for a tired sailor who's glad to be home?"

Sigsbee laughed:

"Tired, are you, Ed? Are we working you too hard?" Sigsbee joked with his old friend.

Palmer chuckled: "No, not really. I just thought I'd try for a little sympathy—it didn't work, did it?"

Sigsbee laughed and shook his head.

"Actually, Ed, you did a great job, especially with that straggler on the way home. The U-boat didn't want to play, eh?"

"Right. I suppose he first thought he had a sitting duck with the troopship, but when we came out from behind it, he didn't want to tangle with a well-armed destroyer. He was submerged and stopped, just watching us. I aimed my bow at him so if he DID shoot, we'd be a hard target, and we watched him as he watched us. He blinked first and left the area."

Sigsbee laughed:

"Just like in the old west!"

Ed joked in return: "…And don't you forget it, Pard!"

"Well, Ed, go ahead with generous liberty for your crew for the next week or so. We'll get you restocked and have you ready for the next round."

"Any idea what the next round might be?"

Sigsbee looked mysterious:

"Hmm—I just might…"

Sigsbee looked at his watch:

"Come on, Ed, and I'll buy you lunch at the O-Club."

Tuesday
December 15, 1942
0930
Lecture Hall
Naval War College

Ed's "free" lunch with Stu Sigsbee on December 8 turned out to be not so "free" after all: the result of that lunch was Ed now approaching the lectern in the crowded main lecture hall at the War College—as the speaker!

At lunch that day a week ago Sigsbee had explained his mysterious look:

"Ed, you have by far the most experience with the hedgehog and I think it's important that the other ship's commanders learn from your experience. As a result…" he paused with a smile, "…I have scheduled you to give a lecture on your experiences at the College next Tuesday."

Ed was stunned. It took him a minute to digest what Sigsbee had just said and, when he did, it gave him mental—and physical—indigestion:

"What?! Me? Give a lecture? Are you crazy?"

Sigsbee retained his grin:

"No, old pal, I'm not crazy and you don't have to give a Nobel Prize-quality talk. Just tell the others what you've experienced and what you've learned. It'll be a piece of cake!"

"Hah! 'Piece of cake'? Oh, sure!"

Sigsbee turned serious:

"Ed, it's important and, as the commander of a warship, you give talks and lectures all the time to your crew. This isn't much different and your audience will be your fellow ship's captains. I know you'll do fine! Besides, don't try to make a formal lecture of it—just get up there and tell the guys what they need to know."

Palmer spent the next several days collecting and organizing his thoughts. As he considered his assignment, he reluctantly came to agree that it probably was a good idea and could be helpful to the others.

On that fateful Tuesday morning, as he left the ship, he encountered Lieutenant Junior Grade Radcliff and he had a sudden flash of inspiration. He hailed Radcliff as they left the ship:

"Mr. Radcliff, may I have a word, please?"

Radcliff hurried and caught up to Palmer:

"Mr. Radcliff, may I ask your destination?"

Prof was startled by the question:

"Uh, Captain, I'm on my way to the War College…"

"I see. And why, may I ask, are you headed for the War College?"

Radcliff smiled:

"Sir, my girlfriend works there. She's a Research Assistant with Dr. Stalling."

"I see. Mr. Radcliff, could you alter your plan slightly? You see, I, too, am on my way to the War College—to give a lecture on our experiences with the hedgehog, and I would really appreciate having you nearby if I face any difficult technical questions. Would you mind?"

Radcliff smiled:

"Actually, sir," Radcliff chuckled, "I am aware of your lecture, and my friend and I had already planned to attend."

Ed was relieved:

"Ah, ha! Well, just stay close in case I need you!"

So there he stood, gazing out across the sea of faces, some he recognized and others he did not. He took a deep breath and started speaking. After he'd been going for just a couple of minutes he found himself relaxing and he realized it wasn't hard to talk about something he knew about. From that point on, the talk went smoothly and lasted for more than 60 minutes. As he finished, he asked if there were any questions—to his surprise, hands shot up throughout the auditorium. After the first few questions, he noted that most dealt with tactics, approaches, timing, communications, and coordination with the gunners and depth charge crews. He realized he had available an expert in the field:

"Gentlemen, if I might pause for just a moment—I have with me today a man who is well-qualified to assist me in answering your questions: Lieutenant Radcliff, would you join me at the podium, please?"

Radcliff was not surprised at the summons—Lucinda was:

"George? What...?"

"It's OK. I direct the Ops Center and I can help answer these questions. I'll be right back." As he stood to go up front, the look of admiration and pride in Lucinda's eyes filled him with confidence.

The "next few minutes" stretched into nearly 45 minutes of detailed questions, answers, and discussions regarding the latest in anti-submarine warfare equipment and tactics. Ed's talk was a resounding success.

The next day, Ed was again in Sigsbee's office:

"Ed—great job yesterday!"

"Thanks, Stu. It wasn't really so bad once I got going..."

Sigsbee nodded:

"Ed, that JG—Radcliff? He seems like an especially competent officer."

Ed nodded in agreement.

"You probably know that ASWORG, down in New York, would love to get their hands on him."

Ed shuddered:

"Oh, not that! Stu, he's pretty much single-handedly designed how the Ops Center works and he runs it flawlessly. Please—don't take him!"

Sigsbee looked at Ed:

"I know, Ed, and I have a way for you to keep him."

Ed looked hopefully at him:

"Ed, the other ships from the hunter group experiment will be arriving here tomorrow. The really great news is, we finally have one of the new escort carriers to work with—the USS *Bogue.* She's just finished her shakedown and is on her way to Norfolk to build the first true hunter-killer group and *Woodside* and your four sister ships are being assigned to her."

Ed was overjoyed:

"Holy cow! That's the best news I've heard in a long time! When do we leave?"

Sigsbee grinned:

"Well, the frosting on the cake is—you leave on Monday, December 28. You get Christmas here at home!"

Ed was bursting to share the news with his men.

Monday
January 4, 1943
USS *Woodside* (DD-203)
Enroute to Norfolk Naval Station

Lieutenant Flynn Boyd had the 4 PM to 8 PM Bridge watch and he was standing at the front of the bridge with his arms resting on the windshield coaming, watching the ship's bow knife through the gentle ocean swells. He was thinking of the events of the past two weeks. Commander Palmer had returned to the ship from the Newport Headquarters and he had immediately gathered all the officers. He reported on the formation of the new "Hunter-Killer Group" and stated *Woodside* and her sister ships were part of it and would be leaving for Norfolk right after the holidays to join with their assigned aircraft carrier. That is exactly what happened and here they were, about halfway to Norfolk, with the other four ships in company. As *Woodside*'s Communication Officer, Boyd anticipated he would soon find himself in the thick of the activities of forming the group.

Boyd was daydreaming when he was startled by Radcliff's voice:

"It's a big ocean, isn't it?"

Boyd smiled:

"Yep. And we just keep seeing more and more of it! What's up, Prof?"

"I've been thinking about the killer group finally coming together, and having an aircraft carrier should make all the difference. I expect you and I will be working increasingly closely and I was wondering if, after you get off watch, we might get together in the Ops Center and talk for a while…"

Boyd had planned to go to his compartment and read, but he quickly decided that was not important:

"Sure, Prof—sounds like a good idea. I'll be relieved in about 45 minutes and I'll come right in."

After Boyd handed off to the oncoming watch, he entered the Ops Center and found that Radcliff had just come in with two steaming mugs of coffee—he offered one to Boyd.

"Thanks, Prof—so, what are you thinking?"

"Well, it seems obvious that our making coordinated attacks on the U-boats requires split-second communication, but it also seems that the plotting table here will be crucial to our being able to keep track of where everybody is. I think we will be two very busy fellows!"

Boyd nodded in agreement.

Radcliff continued:

"When I was hanging around at ASWORG, they mentioned the British had come up with something they call 'High-Frequency Direction Finding'." He chuckled: "They call it 'huff-duff'."

Boyd smiled.

"It seems the U-boats are controlled directly from their headquarters ashore—they are directed where to go and when to go there. Also, the boats are required to frequently report their location. The result is a lot of radio chatter and the British have figured out a way to listen in and then triangulate the location of each U-boat."

"Wow! They really can do that?"

"Yes. If I could have a late Christmas gift, it would be to have one of those huff-duff receivers!"

"But doesn't our radar do just as well?"

Radcliff answered thoughtfully:

"Yes, but it sure wouldn't hurt to have a second way of finding them!"

Boyd was excited:

"The combination of this 'huff-duff'-thing with radar, sonar, the hedgehog, depth charges, and now airplanes, would give us a chance to really hurt the U-boats!"

"Exactly! I think, between the two of us, when we get to Norfolk, we should keep our ears open and make every effort to get one of those units."

"I'm in!"

They went on to discuss ways to better coordinate their efforts in the Ops Room, ways that would soon pay off.

* * * * * * * *

Woodside and her small task group arrived at Norfolk the next morning and were directed to anchor in Hampton Roads near where *Bogue* was tied to Pier Two. Ed's group consisted of *Woodside* and the familiar ships from their earlier abortive attack group experiment:

> *USS Christie* (Lt. Cmdr. Myles Boyden)
> *USS Nickle*   (Lt. Cmdr. Jackson Woodley)
> *USS Loren*   (Lt. Cmdr. Anthony Joseph)
> *USS Ashton* (Lt. Cmdr. Stephen Lawler)

Ed and his fellow captains were summoned to an important meeting aboard *Bogue* at 1500 hours. They arrived a few minutes early and were shown to a corner of the ship's expansive hangar deck where chairs and a chalkboard had been set up. They talked quietly until a group of *Bogue's* officers arrived, led by a Captain.

A Lieutenant stepped to the front and motioned for quiet:

"Thank you, gentlemen, for coming. We have a vitally important mission ahead of us and we want to assure the greatest possible coordination and success. Gentlemen, I introduce the Captain of *Bogue*, Captain Giles Short."

The stocky, serious-appearing Captain strode to the lectern:

"Men, as you know, we have been selected to form the first hunter-killer group and our orders are simple: sink every U-boat we encounter! I am aware of your background and training in making coordinated attacks on enemy submarines, and we are now in a position to make strides far beyond that rudimentary experiment."

Hearing their earlier efforts described as "rudimentary" made Ed's hackles rise.

The Captain continued:

"Men, your job as destroyers in this group is to protect the aircraft carrier…"

When Ed heard that, his head snapped around to look with concern at Tony Joseph sitting next to him, who looked startled.

The Captain went on to describe in glowing terms how the addition of aircraft to the fight at sea would make all the difference and he expressed his confidence that *Bogue* would soon be at the pinnacle of ridding U-boats from the Atlantic. He finished speaking and a Commander, the Executive Officer of the carrier, walked to the chalkboard and began describing ship placements while underway:

"Gentlemen, you will serve as escorts to *Bogue*, and you will be placed in position here—and here—and here—and here." He sketched destroyers placed one in front, one on either side and one behind the carrier. "The fifth destroyer will roam around the group as added protection. You will be placed 1000 yards from the carrier and you will maintain that position at all times."

That was all Ed could stand—his hand shot up:

"Yes, Commander?"

Ed spoke firmly:

"Commander, hard and painful experience has taught us that escorting at such close range is useless. We..."

The Commander interrupted: "'Useless'? You are saying close escort is 'useless'? That's preposterous!"

Ed barely contained his anger:

"That is correct—useless! The British began the war escorting the convoys close-aboard and the convoys were decimated! We had the same experience. An escort placed only 1000 yards away is of no value at stopping a submerged attack—the sub can easily fire from 3000 yards or more with ease. Escorting too close simply gives the submarine more easy targets!"

The Commander responded acidly: "And what do you suggest?"

"Practical experience has shown that maintaining a range of at least 4000 yards is optimum."

"Four thousand yards! That's ludicrous!"

Ed started to respond hotly, but the Captain interceded:

"Now, gentlemen, let's maintain a civil discussion! We'll discuss these details more later. Please continue, Commander Levin."

The Commander went on to describe general communication protocols and then he sat down. He was glowering. A Lieutenant wearing aviator's wings stepped to the front:

"I'm sure," he smiled, "that we all agree that the addition of aviation to the response to the U-boats is an important adjunct. I am convinced that aviation will make all the difference—you fellows protect the carrier and we will take care of the U-boats!"

Ed shook his head and Steve Lawler nearly jumped out of his seat. The Lieutenant noticed the strongly negative response to his statements:

"It appears you men disagree with that?'

Ed stood, breathing deeply to control his anger and disappointment:

"Yes, Lieutenant, with all due respect, we disagree. There is no doubt that the inclusion of airborne scouting and attacks is a vital piece of our tactics, but to blithely assume that an airplane can do it all is…" Ed paused to find the right words, "…misplaced over-confidence."

"Misplaced over-confidence? Why else do you think we're here? Scouting? Is that all we are? We…"

Ed held up his hand: "Sir, please hear me out. No, not just scouting—your airplane can find a surfaced U-boat and attack it far beyond the ships of the attack group. That is a vital capability that has been missing from the central North Atlantic. However, the U-boats do not simply sit on the surface enjoying the warm sunshine while you fly over and bomb them. Are you able to locate a submerged submarine? Are you able to find a surfaced submarine on a dark and stormy night? And, I'm sure you realize that the U-boat will shoot back at you—usually quite accurately?"

Ed paused. Then:

"Gentlemen, it has been my understanding that the formation of this specialized attack group has two entrenched reasons: one is to 'hunt' the U-boats, and the other is to 'kill' the U-boats we find. You have vital elements to help make that happen—but we, too, have vital, hard-learned experience to contribute."

The Lieutenant snorted:

"And how many U-boats has your old tub destroyed?"

Ed smiled: "*Woodside* has five confirmed destructions and two probables. How many have you sunk, Lieutenant?"

Ed's compatriots smiled; the Captain again interceded:

"Well, Lieutenant Wilson," he smiled, "I think he's got you there! But the point is an important one—it seems our mutual pride in our specialty areas is causing friction. Would you agree, Commander Palmer?"

Ed nodded: "Yes, Captain, I agree. Both aviation and seaborne weapons have much to add to the goal of sinking U-boats. Success will not be accomplished by just skilled destroyers finding and attacking the enemy, nor will it be accomplished by just the use of aviation—it will be accomplished by the closely coordinated use of all the weapons at our disposal, ships AND airplanes."

The group was quiet. Then the Captain spoke:

"Commander Palmer, that was well-said. Perhaps our enthusiasm has blinded us to the most effective manner in which to utilize our resources. I propose that our path going forward is one of 'we' rather than of 'us and them'." He looked at his officers questioningly: "Gentlemen?"

With some reluctance, they slowly nodded their agreement. He then looked at Ed and his men: "Gentlemen?"

Also with some reluctance, they nodded their agreement.

"Good! Then, tomorrow morning at 0900 we will reconvene here to establish the details of how WE will vanquish the enemy. Until tomorrow..." He walked away and his officers followed him.

Ed and his compatriots stood and headed for the gangway. Just before they reached the quarterdeck, Ed was approached by an Ensign:

"Commander Palmer?"

Ed nodded.

"Sir, the Captain would like you to join him in his cabin."

Ed grimaced inwardly, but nodded at the young officer:

"Fine—lead the way."

When they reached the Captain's cabin, the Ensign announced Ed and then departed.

"Commander Palmer, come in, please. Have a seat. Coffee?"

Well, Ed thought to himself, *he's trying to be nice, so I will, too.*

"Yes, Captain, that would be nice. Thank you."

"Commander, it seems our teams got off to a bit of a rocky start. I think that's too bad and I hope we can remedy that."

Ed nodded in agreement.

"I do think," the Captain continued, "that what we are seeing is a reflection of the level of excitement regarding our role."

"I agree."

"Please share with me your experiences fighting our formidable foe…"

Ed launched into his experiences, beginning with the first time of "accompanying" an England-bound convoy that had no escort at all for the first two-thirds of the voyage and continuing his description right up to their recent experiences using the hedgehog to destroy the submarines. Captain Short listened closely. When Ed finished, Captain Short was quiet for a few moments before he spoke:

"Commander, you do, indeed, have a remarkable depth of experience. That just makes it more crucial that we forge our teams into a single-minded, highly effective, anti-submarine group. I suggest we focus on the goal—find 'em and sink 'em!"

Ed smiled in agreement. He then shared a thought that he hoped might be helpful:

"Captain, on each of our ships, we have established an 'Operations Center' that collects and coordinates all information regarding any contacts and our attacks. It includes information from radar, sonar, radio, lookouts—everything. It has proven invaluable."

Captain Short was thoughtful:

"Hmm. That sounds brilliant--would it be possible to have some of my people come over and tour your Center and talk with your people? Your guys could show us how it's done."

Ed smiled: "It would be a pleasure!"

The men continued talking for another half-hour and both were inwardly relieved that they were beginning to respect each other and to look forward to working together.

Wednesday
January 6, 1943
0900
Hangar Deck
USS Bogue (ACV-9)

The group reconvened as directed. The destroyer people and the carrier people initially were standoffish to one another, but Ed made a point of approaching Commander Levin:

"Good morning, Commander—how are you this fine morning?"

Levin noted Ed's obvious attempt at being friendly and decided to respond in kind:

"I'm fine, Commander—and you?"

Ed laughed:

"I'm fine—but if we keep on talking this way we'll soon be sending formal notes across the table! I'm happy to be here and I look forward to hashing out the best ways of getting those U-boats."

Levin laughed:

"Yes, I guess we have been a bit formal. Your name is Ed—correct?"

'Yes."

"Mine is Mark. I'm happy to meet you, Ed."

"And I you, Mark."

The men shook hands and both groups noted their smiles and their handshake. Things began to thaw after that.

Captain Short entered and things got busy very quickly. He started the morning by sharing some of the things he and Ed had discussed the day before. He then described his ideas regarding how to find, track, and attack the enemy U-boats. His comments struck Ed as balanced and thoughtful and he was encouraged. The morning continued and the discussions became increasingly detailed. The men began to work together and, soon, were enthusiastically sharing ideas and suggestions.

The group broke for lunch and talk around the various tables was animated and congenial. When they got back together, Captain Short asked Ed to describe *Woodside's* Operations Center and the carrier men were quite interested. They noted that the Ops Center sounded like what the larger ships were forming and calling the "Combat Information Center"—or "CIC". They jumped at Ed's offer to visit *Woodside* the next morning.

Upon his return to his ship, Ed quickly rounded up LTJG Radcliff, Ensign Boyd, and several of the technicians and told them of the pending visit. *Woodside's* team quickly huddled and soon felt they were ready to make a cohesive display of how the center functioned. It was agreed that "Prof" Radcliff would be the main guide and speaker.

* * * * * * * *

Arriving a few minutes before 0900 the next morning, the boat carrying *Bogue's* people brought four officers and two enlisted technicians to *Woodside's* quarterdeck. The group was ushered up to the bridge and into the Ops Center where Radcliff and his team were waiting. Following introductions and the provision of the ever-present coffee and rolls, Radcliff bid everyone to be seated and he began his presentation.

Radcliff's past as a trained educator quickly became apparent as he started by first describing his meetings with Professor Stalling and his team at the War College, and then his subsequent meetings with the people at ASWORG. Sharing this background established Radcliff's credibility and also provided the foundation for the design and function of *Woodside's* Ops Center. He went on to describe in detail how information is generated and processed as quickly and accurately as possible. He stressed the need to have the essential technologies in close proximity— radar, sonar, and nearby radio—and the means to immediately coordinate and plot the incoming information. The *Woodside* team then acted out a typical scenario of finding, tracking, and attacking a U-boat. The men from *Bogue* watched and listened carefully. When Radcliff finished his talk, he asked for questions and comments—and that is when the meeting really became intense.

The sonar operator from the carrier described the difference in how his contacts were treated:

"When I get a contact, I tell the bridge and they immediately turn away from it. When you get a contact, your ship immediately turns toward it. You see the U-boat as a target—we see our carrier as the target!"

Wirtz smiled. Radcliff responded:

"That's one of the key differences—we are the hunter. That's not to say that at times we've also been the hunted—we've dodged our fair share of torpedoes!"

After numerous other questions and comments, a Lieutenant from *Bogue* spoke:

"Fellows, you've done a fine job here. Perhaps I might make a suggestion to make it even better: while I served aboard *Lexington*, we installed a vertical piece of clear Plexiglas for plotting the contacts and movements. It took less space than your plotting table and it could be read from either side."

Radcliff lit up with a big smile:

"Yes! What a great idea! And if we mount it properly, it could be seen from the bridge through the open door. The captain wouldn't have to keep leaving the bridge to see the developing situation. What a great suggestion!"

The visitors were invited to lunch in the wardroom and the conversation was animated and friendly. Teamwork had blossomed.

Monday
January 11, 1943
Norfolk Naval Station

On the Monday morning following the team discussions, Prof and Boyd headed ashore to try to find some Plexiglas. Joey asked if he could tag along and the others didn't mind. They rode the ship's boat to fleet landing and then set off on their quest.

Prof took the lead:

"Guys, I think our best bet is the supply center and I'll bet that huge building over there is it." He pointed to a large, rectangular, multi-storied building several blocks away that looked like a giant warehouse. They arrived and it turned out the building was, indeed, the Naval Supply Center. It was a huge place and they wondered where to begin.

On the end of the building was a double-door with the legend NSC overhead.

"Hmm," Prof wondered, "maybe that's the front door."

That seemed as good a guess as any, so they went in. What they encountered was a desk manned by a stout First Class Petty Officer who looked up when they entered:

"What do you need, men?"

Prof spoke up: "We're from USS *Woodside*, anchored out in the Roads, and we need a sheet of Plexiglas."

The PO held out his hand:

"Let's see your requisition."

Prof stammered in return:

"Uh, well, we don't have one yet. We're trying to find out where we might get some Plexiglas, then we'll fill out the requisition."

The PO looked stern:

"Nope. Sorry, sir, but without a requisition, I can't help you."

Prof wasn't about to give up so easily:

"Do you have Plexiglas here? Is it available from this center?"

The sailor shook his head: "I don't know Plexiglas from a beer glass—but without a requisition, you can't get nothin'."

It seemed they were stymied. Prof was pretty sure the supply center would have Plexiglas sheets, but it looked like getting one would take an act of congress. He motioned to the others to join him outside:

"OK, guys—two can play this game. Instead of going all the way back out to *Woodside,* let's go over to *Bogue* and try to find that Lieutenant. Maybe he knows if they have the material here and maybe he can give us some specifics on sizes and stuff—and maybe even a blank requisition form."

As they hiked over to Pier Two, Prof asked if anyone remembered the Lieutenant's name.

Joey smiled:

"Bailey—I remember because I had a teacher named Bailey."

Prof grinned:

"Well, Joey, you just earned your keep! Let's go find him."

When they reached the pier, they climbed the brow and crossed to the quarterdeck. After appropriate salutes, they identified themselves and asked for Lieutenant Bailey.

The Officer of the Deck told the sailor on watch to find Lieutenant Bailey and ask him to come to the quarterdeck. The sailor disappeared and, after a ten-minute wait, he returned with Bailey.

"Well, hello, fellows—this is a surprise! What brings you here?"

Prof described their problem and Bailey smiled:

"Yes, I've encountered that same PO and had the same sort of problem." He was about to invite them to the wardroom to talk when he realized Joey was with them. Instead:

"Men, why don't we step into the hangar deck where we can talk."

Once there, Prof asked for specifics about the Plexiglas—size, thickness, etc. Bailey was quick to answer and, as he finished, he smiled:

"…And don't forget a supply of grease pencils. We used different-colored ones for different targets."

When asked about the requisition form, he asked them to wait and he went off, returning a few minutes later with a form. He had already arranged to have the specifics typed in and it was even signed. Prof laughed:

"This is wonderful, but I suppose I shouldn't ask about the signature?"

Bailey just smiled.

The men returned to NSC and presented the requisition to the PO. He read it carefully, stamped it, and tore off the top sheet, placing it in a basket that passed through the wall. He gave Prof the bottom sheet.

"Sir, you guys might want to get to some lunch and then come back. Then take your paper to the first loading dock on the side down there—pointing to the southern side of the building—and give it to the guy there. He should have your—whatever it is—ready for you."

They thanked him and they did, indeed, enjoy a nice lunch at the base café.

Getting the unwieldy sheet back to *Woodside* was challenging, especially on the boat ride to the ship—it nearly blew out of Joey's hands, but Boyd was quick to grab it and help steady it. And, yes, they did remember the cryptically–marked "Grease Pencils, colored, assorted, qty: 1 doz".

*　*　*　*　*　*　*　*

The next days and weeks were busy: *Bogue* was receiving the installation of modern 5"/38 guns and many additional 40MM antiaircraft weapons. Her fire protection systems were modernized, also. Things were humming on *Woodside* as well…

When Prof and his helpers got back to the ship, they took the Plexiglas up to the Ops Center and began figuring the best place to mount it. They asked Captain Palmer to come and give his opinion regarding the most useful mounting location and orientation:

"Fellows," he said, "having it where I can see it through the doorway is great. I wouldn't normally want to leave that door open, but it's not a watertight door and it doesn't provide any real protection for the Ops Center, so—yes, let's hang it where it can be seen easily from the bridge. Prof, could one of you men hold it somewhat in place?"

Joey held it up, facing the open door.

"Yes, that's the right spot—how about a foot higher?" He looked carefully; "Yes—right there! Can you mark that position somehow?"

Prof had a tape measure and he quickly noted the height and placement.

"Thanks, Captain!"

It turned out the installation of the Plexiglas inspired many other improvements in the Center. First, they asked a Machinist's Mate to suggest how to mount the sheet and he took over that project. They discussed how to mark the sheet and learned of a Yeoman who is an artist. He was approached and asked about somehow marking the range and direction markings that were needed—and he quickly took over that task. Once the old plotting table was removed, all of those who serve in the Center were gathered and asked about improving the placement of equipment and furniture. Wirtz stated that, at busy times, the room became so noisy he had difficulty hearing the sonar and hydrophones. It was finally agreed to enlarge the present small sound booth into formal surrounding walls covered with sound-deadening material. Wirtz took over that project and had Joey help him. A huge improvement came when an Electrician's Mate was asked about somehow installing a dedicated sound-powered system for the Center. He and some communication specialist friends jumped at the chance and soon, the Ops Center had its own sound-powered communication system—no more yelling to report contacts! The Ops center was a busy place for several days as it was reconfigured, modernized, and improved. And at the center of it all was the vertical Plexiglas sheet with range and distance circles painted neatly on it, ready to track enemy submarines, ships, and aircraft.

While the work on *Woodside* continued, *Bogue* completed her upgrades and began underway anti-submarine training with her embarked squadrons. They remained in the general Norfolk area and the exercises kept all of her men very busy as they developed and practiced their attack procedures. *Woodside* steamed out several times to accompany the carrier and to practice coordination. It was generally very beneficial, although Ed and his men were still sometimes frustrated at the "aircraft will stop the subs" mentality. At least they were able to test and refine the improved Ops Center.

Monday
February 1, 1943
USS Woodside (DD-203)
At Sea Near Norfolk

During the time the various improvements were being installed on the ships, Ed had been keeping in close communication with the captains of the other destroyers in the group. They, too, had been meeting together to design search and attack procedures based upon updating their earlier training and experiences and now including the availability of aircraft. They reached a point where they wanted to go to sea to practice and Ed agreed. They went to sea on Monday morning, February 1.

Ed set things up so that, at first, *Woodside* played the role of a surfaced submarine and the other ships practiced their coordinated attacks. It was great practice and, as communication procedures improved, the attackers became much more proficient. Then they switched and one of the other ships played the role of enemy. They ended up remaining at sea for three days and they were pleased when, on the third day, *Bogue* steamed out to join them. It was a busy time, but coordination rapidly improved. It also proved that the revised Ops Center was even more effective than it had been originally. As the Group steamed back to port late in the afternoon of Wednesday, February 3, everyone was eager to rejoin the war.

* * * * * * * *

During the third week of February, the supply barges began coming thick and fast to feed and fuel the many ships out in

Hampton Roads. *Woodside* and her mates were at the top of the list—they had just learned the *Bogue* group would be leaving on February 24 to head for Argentia.

The transit northward was uneventful and arrival at Argentia on February 28 was unexceptional for *Woodside* and her sisters, but it was the first time *Bogue* had called at the vital northern base. It would not be the last.

On Friday, March 5, *Bogue* and her escorts set sail, and on the 6th met convoy HX-228, bound for Liverpool. The convoy was a large one, originally including a total of 87 merchant ships and 21 escorts. Those numbers began to change quickly—fifteen of the merchants were soon ordered back to Halifax for various reasons and there were also two collisions, one involving two ships and another involving three ships. All returned slowly to Halifax. Another ship was unable to keep up with the convoy and was sent back to New York City, another returned to New York with shifted cargo, and yet a third turned back to New York because of cracked hull plating. As the days wore on and ships—and escorts—kept dropping by the wayside, Ed shook his head at the woeful changes that had taken place since *Woodside's* last convoy back in August. The number of U-boats reported at sea had soared and the number of ship sinkings had climbed to astronomical levels—it seemed that things in the North Atlantic were at a point of catastrophe.

The convoy slogged along and the hunter-killer group stayed with them—which Ed thought was a mistake. He believed the group should be scouting ahead of the convoy so they could find and attack the U-boats that were sure to be there. Admittedly, the carrier flew off regular patrols but, so far, no submarines had been located. Finally, on the morning of Wednesday, March 10, one of *Bogue's* aircraft located and attacked—or tried to attack—a surfaced U-boat. Unfortunately, the attack failed when the airplane's depth bombs failed to release. That afternoon, *Bogue* and her group were detached from HX-228 and ordered to return to Argentia—with one exception: due to her extensive experience and modern electronics, *Woodside* was detached from the group and told to remain with the convoy, staying with them all the way to Liverpool. Ed requested, and was allowed, to scout far ahead of the convoy, using her radar and sonar to locate enemy submarines. It didn't take long…

According to a British Admiralty message forwarded to *Woodside* by the convoy commander, 17 U-boats were awaiting the arrival of HX-228! The convoy was large and unwieldy, and the reduced number of escorts were still staying close by the convoy—which led Ed to expect that little help would be available when *Woodside* plowed into the waiting subs—but he didn't hesitate. Ed commented to his officers that "more U-boats means we have more targets"—they didn't smile at the pronouncement.

The first contact hit the radar screen at 23:21 hours:

"Plot—Radar: contact bearing 015 degrees, 35000 yards. Probable surfaced submarine."

The plot was noted on the Plexiglas "Plotting Board"—using a red grease pen to denote an enemy submarine. Already plotted was a general green grouping behind *Woodside* denoting the friendly ships of the convoy.

"Plot—Radar: contact now bears 018, distance 32000." The mark was entered on the board.

After a few minutes, Ed had arrived on the bridge and took a glance at the board. Seeing the single contact still miles ahead of his ship, he decided to delay calling General Quarters for a few more minutes.

"Whoa! Plot—Radar: a new contact bearing 010, 34000 yards! Original contact bears 020, 30000 yards." The corresponding marks were made on the board. Ed loved being able to see exactly what was happening directly from the bridge. With the advent of the second contact, Ed ordered GQ and the alarm bells rang throughout the ship.

As the minutes passed, additional contacts were made until a total of five probable submarines were noted, stretched in a line running roughly east-west along the present course of the convoy. Ed notified both the convoy commander and the escort commander, suggesting they alter course to the south.

Ed was standing in the doorway, looking thoughtfully at the plot. Prof walked over and smiled:

"Well, Captain, that's a bunch of them! And there are supposed to be even more somewhere out there. Will we be altering course to block them from the convoy?"

Ed looked sharply at him:

"Alter course? As in 'let's get out of here'? No, sir—not a chance! Our job is to sink U-boats and we're going to do just that!"

The others on the bridge overhead the conversation and, upon hearing Ed's response, looked at each other in alarm.

Ed was aware of their reaction, but he knew *Woodside* could attack successfully if they approached it correctly. Ed shook his head: *They think I've gone nuts and I'm obsessed with sinking subs. I'm not stupid, but we WILL do our job—and live to tell about it!*

"Talker: Notify the guns to be prepared to fire on my order. Tell the gun boss about the positions of the subs. We will not be using any star shells—there is plenty of moonlight to see the targets. I want to attack as many of the subs simultaneously as possible, so assign each gun a specific target. We'll be passing down their line behind the subs so their deck guns can't bear on us. Notify the hedgehog team to prepare to fire the minute any of those subs submerges, and I want perfect coordination between the hedgehog team and the depth charge teams back aft. Torpedomen, stay alert! Alert everyone that things are about to get very noisy and very busy. Helm—be ready for instantaneous helm orders."

"Engineroom—all ahead flank!"

Joey was assisting Wirtz on sonar and when he heard the Captain, he couldn't help but smile nervously. He looked at Wirtz:

"Wow! Here we go!"

As the range closed, Ed positioned *Woodside* to pass behind the subs at a distance of about 500 yards. As they neared, everyone topside could clearly see the first sub in the line and the next one

41

along appeared as a distant shadow. Just as Ed was about to order his guns to fire, the first submarine obviously knew they were coming and beat him to it—their rear-facing antiaircraft guns opened up on *Woodside.*

"Guns—open fire!"

The racket was stunning—*Woodside's* 3-inchers cracking, the sub's machineguns chattering, and even *Woodside's* aft-mounted 40MM was whooping away. Gun #1 was firing at the distant target, Gun #2 was firing at the nearer one, and the 40MM was scoring hits on the near one. There was a rattling sound as the submarine's shells struck *Woodside* along the port side.

As *Woodside* drew abreast of the first sub, the second one was much easier to see, and the third one was now a shadow in the distance. Alerted by the first U-boat, the others were scrambling to get underway. Griffin Stone on radar noted the sub's movements and reported them to the plotter.

As *Woodside* raced along the line of enemy vessels, Ed was carefully monitoring their position relative to the subs—if they got too close, the ship's guns would not be able to depress far enough, but if they were too far out the sub's torpedoes would have enough run to arm and *Woodside* would be an easy target.

Wednesday
March 10, 1943
21:53
U-115

Kapitanleutnant Heinz Folger was angry:

"Berger! How could this attack happen? Where are the lookouts? Why did we not hear that ship coming? This is unacceptable!"

Helmut Berger, First Watch Officer and second in command of U-115 was not surprised at his captain's anger—it seemed that nearly everything lately made his captain angry. This was their first war patrol after a lengthy refit period at the submarine base at St. Nazaire, France, and Folger's hyperactive sense of Nazi dominance had overcome any rational sense.

Berger ignored the man's outburst:

"Sir, we are now underway and building speed. We are the third boat in the line and the enemy's shells are falling behind us. We should be able to get away in the dark."

"Get away?! We are not running away, Berger! As the enemy ship passes behind us we will gain enough range and we will fire our stern torpedo at him. That will be the end of this impudent intruder!"

Folger was unhappy when his lookouts reported that the enemy ship was turning to maintain its close range to the U-115.

"Well, then," he stormed, "we will sink him with our guns. Berger, you tell those gunners that if they fail to severely damage this enemy ship, they will be sent to the Russian front!"

Berger grimaced—he knew all too well that Folger meant what he said. Morale among the crew was low because of earlier reprisals Folger had taken against crewmen he felt had underperformed.

As U-115 built speed, the enemy destroyer was closing the range. The enemy was firing at each of the boats rather than concentrating its fire on any single boat. They seemed to be making hits and causing damage to the other submarines and Berger fully intended to bring the attack to a halt.

"Aft guns—open fire!"

Thursday
March 11, 1943
00:06
USS Woodside (DD 203)

Woodside was taking hits from the rear guns of the two subs they had passed so far. They were of smaller caliber than the large deck guns carried ahead of the conning tower, but they were still doing damage. As *Woodside* raced along the line of U-boats, all of her portside guns were fully engaged in striking the boats as they passed. The third one was now within range and Gun #1 shifted to take it under fire. The rear gun of the submarine began firing and, as *Woodside* raced closer, the German gunners seemed to be targeting the destroyer's bridge. Suddenly there were sparks and zings of shells striking the forward and port side all around where Ed and his men ducked for cover.

"Helm—maintain this distance from the subs! Guns—see if you can silence that gun mount!"

As *Woodside* came even with the sub, two things happened within moments of each other…

Folger watched with glee as his gunners pounded the bridge area of the oncoming destroyer:

"Good! Good! Keep it up! That should make them think twice about attacking my boat!"

A moment later, a 3" shell from *Woodside* struck the lower port side of U-115's conning tower, resulting in a deafening blast and a jolt that rocked the submarine. It was followed seconds later by another that wiped off the periscope shears and showered the men on the conning tower with shrapnel-like debris. Folger gasped:

Berger looked and saw his captain clinging weakly to the bridge coaming, blood streaming down his face.

"Kapitan! You are injured!" Berger rushed to assist his wounded leader.

Folger shook his head and forced himself to stand upright:

"Ach! It is nothing, Berger, I am all right." He had been slashed by a piece of debris and was bleeding heavily from his forehead.

Berger helped Folger to a corner of the con and pulled off his shirt to press against the wound to slow or stop the bleeding.

"Berger, is the boat damaged?"

"We have been hit, but I do not yet know the extent of the damage."

Thursday
March 11, 1943
00:11
USS Woodside (DD-203)

Captain Palmer had just issued his order to the guns when, suddenly, the glass of the bridge shattered and knife-edged shards raged through the enclosed space. The bridge-talker cried out and dropped to his knees. The Coxswain grunted in pain but remained at his post. Ed heard the bullets entering with the sound of hundreds of stinging wasps and then felt a jolt and a sharp pain in his neck. He began to feel woozy.

Prof was in the Ops Room when the bridge was hit and he rushed into the bridge and immediately saw the damage and the injured men. He ordered the Ops Center plotter to call for the medical Corpsman on the double. He then saw Captain Palmer, slowing sinking into his Captain's chair, covered in blood.

"Captain—where are you hit?!" He looked closely and could see the man's neck wound. He grabbed from his pocket the rag he normally used as an eraser on the plot board and pressed it against the Captain's wound.

Woodside continued ahead and the rear 40 MM mount could finally bear on the submarine. Mike Torelli aimed for the sub's rear gun and squeezed his triggers. A hail of 40 MM shells struck around the sub's gun and, a moment later, that gun went silent.

Thursday
March 11, 1943
00:13
U-115

"Berger! Why has our gun stopped firing?"

"Sir, the destroyer silenced it. We must get away from here!"

Folger growled in frustration:

"Can we submerge?"

"I think so. The big shell blasted a huge hole in the side of the conning tower, but I think we can go below and close the conning tower hatch. We should be able to submerge then."

Folger gave his permission and Berger helped him to get down through the conning tower and into the control room below. The remaining topside crewmen slithered down and the hatch was securely closed.

"Submerge! Level off at 20 meters!"

Thursday
March 11, 1943
00:15
USS Woodside (DD-203)

As Prof looked around, he noted that the submarine's gun had stopped firing. He also realized he couldn't see the next two subs. Finally, he saw the nearest submarine dropping beneath the waves. He called out to Ops Center:

"Where are the other two subs?"

A voice answered: "They just submerged and this one is going down, too."

"Is this one sinking?"

"No—it sounds like he's submerging."

"Radcliff—what's happening?" Ed's voice was weak.

"Sir, the next two subs have submerged and the near one is, too."

Ed nodded slowly:

"You have to go after those other two or they will sink us." His voice was fading as he lost consciousness, but Prof heard one last, weak, word—"hedgehog".

It seemed that Lieutenant Junior Grade George Radcliff was now in charge of Woodside. OK, he thought, so be it!

He looked at the plot board and was surprised to see that it seemed to give a current picture:

"Carlson—is that plot current?"

"Yes, sir!"

He noted the locations of the two submerged U-boats. They were off to port bearing 350 relative, with the nearest about 2000 yards.

"Helm—come left to 350 relative! Hedgehog, prepare to shoot— and then reload faster than you ever have!"

Woodside was still racing at flank speed and she closed the range to the first submerged U-boat quickly. Prof watched the range close until the sub was 250 yards ahead:

"Fire hedgehog! Prepare to roll depth charges!"

He heard the rapid-fire sound of the hedgehog projectiles being launched and he saw the circle of their splashes. He waited a moment, then:

"Roll depth charges!"

"Sonar, how far to the next sub?"

"1000 yards and closing fast!'

"Keep talking to me!"

"Distance 750 yards, bearing directly in front us. I think we got two hits with the 'hog."

"Distance 500 yards!"

"Distance 250 yards!"

"Fire hedgehog!"

It was a close thing—the hedgehog crew had raced to reload and the last projectile had just been dropped into place when the order came to fire again.

Again, he waited a moment, then:

"Roll depth charges!"

The sea around *Woodside* was erupting from the various explosions. Wirtz, on sonar, couldn't hear a thing.

Radcliff wanted to know where the original three subs were:

"Plot: show me the other three subs!"

The plotter, Seaman Carlson, pointed to the red grease marks:

"Sir, they have all submerged. One is—here, and another is—here, and that third one is—here."

Radcliff noted their positions. He was also aware that *Woodside* had been pretty well shot up:

He looked around the bridge and noticed that there was a new phone-talker, the Coxswain had a bright new bandage on his right leg, and the medical team was tending to the captain. The broken glass and debris had been removed and it was very windy due to the broken windows.

me a damage report!"

ns are functional; four gunners are wounded, none
ne ship has numerous bullet holes, but all are above the
e. Damage control reports we are fully functional."

—any change?"

rtz called out from the Ops Center:

Prof, remember—when we travel this fast I can't really hear
much. For me to hear accurately, we need to slow down."

Prof nodded.

Wirtz continued with a smile: "Sir, from what I can hear, we hit
them pretty good: Target 1 was damaged by gunfire and is
submerged and limping noisily away to the north. Target 2 was
also damaged by gunfire and is also submerged and moving
slowly away northward. Target 3 was hit pretty hard and has
submerged. It's barely moving, generally northward. I think I hear
damage noses. Targets 4 and 5 were struck by the hedgehog—
#4 was hit twice and #5 once. I don't know yet what other
damage might have been done by the depth charges. Both #4
and #5 are continuing slowly towards the north."

Prof was considering what to do next when he heard the
captain's weak voice: "Well done, Mr. Radcliff—but it's time to get
us out of here…"

Prof smiled:

"Sounds good to me, but—I need to know if there're any others out there so I'll know which way to go. Stoney, is there anything on radar—especially to the south?"

Stone called back: "No, my screen is clear. The convoy is behind us to the southwest."

"Thanks. Helm, bring us about to steer 200 degrees true. Reduce speed to full ahead."

He happened to glance at Captain Palmer, slumped in his chair—he was smiling faintly.

Thursday
March 11, 1943
00:20
U-115

As Folger was tended by the medical orderly, Berger took stock of the boat's situation: they had suffered a large hole in the port side of the conning tower and the conning tower was now flooded; there were numerous smaller holes in the outer hull and fuel was pouring out and, worst of all, the periscopes had been destroyed and U-115 was blind while submerged. He had heard the numerous explosions all around them and he assumed the other boats had been the objects of those attacks. He didn't know if any had been sunk and he didn't know if there was anyone left to help should U-115 need assistance. He decided to steer northward to clear the area. When the soundman could no longer hear the destroyer, he would attempt to surface. He gave the orders, and then glanced at Folger, who was frowning. Berger had a thought which he couldn't contain:

"Kapitan, did you notice? That ship was our old friend Number 203…"

Folger grimaced angrily, then slumped unconscious.

Thursday
March 11, 1943
07:35
USS Woodside (DD-203)

Radcliff took *Woodside* clear of the battle area, then slowed down and circled to rejoin the convoy. After Radcliff secured the ship from General Quarters, Lieutenant Bevins, the Executive Officer, came to the bridge and took over command. Radcliff reported to him all the details of what had happened and concluded by noting that Captain Palmer was not seriously injured and he had been taken below to his cabin.

Thursday
March 11, 1943
07:35
U-115

Helmut Berger listened carefully as his soundman described the chaos around them:

"Sir, there are noises all around us. I think the first two boats in the line are damaged, but still under control. They are moving away to the north. The last two boats seem to have been seriously damaged. They are still submerged, but they each are making terrible noises."

Berger asked his Chief Engineer about their propulsion status:

"Sir, the electric motors are undamaged. I don't know for certain, but I think the diesels are unharmed, also. Both shafts seem to be fine, however—our port screw seems to be damaged and it is very noisy."

"And our fuel supply?"

The Chief looked gloomy: "We are losing a great deal of fuel due to the outer blister being holed."

Berger fought a sense of dismay:

"Can we get home?"

The Chief was thoughtful:

"Well, if we use only the starboard shaft and screw, stay on the surface and run at greatly reduced speed, we might come close."

"Close??"

The Chief nodded slowly.

Berger considered their predicament and reached a decision:

"Soundman, can you hear any surface vessels?"

"No."

He then gave the order: "Prepare to surface!"

He hoped they could surface. The damage to the conning tower had flooded it and he hoped that as the tower rose above the surface, it would drain. Other damage was unknown—but he expected they would find out soon…

"Surface!"

The boat responded sluggishly due to the large weight of water in the conning tower. The aft hydroplane operator reported his planes were not responding properly. He thought they might have jammed as he inclined them to surface.

What else can go wrong? Berger bemoaned to himself.

Slowly, U-115 staggered toward the surface. The crew was now aware of the multiplicity of problems and they were looking upward hopefully. Berger smiled—*why are they looking upward? We're down here in this steel tube and they cannot see the surface—I suppose it's just a natural expression of wanting to go up.*

Finally, the tower broke the surface. Berger noted the boat was rolling unnaturally. He paid close attention and detected that the longer the tower was above water, the more normal the roll became. *Ah—must be the water draining out! Good!*

"Sir, the boat is surfaced!"

"Thank you. I want a strong man to slowly open the conning tower hatch—there is probably still much water in there and opening it will result in quite a waterfall. Be careful!"

Indeed, as the hatch was cracked open, water cascaded into the control room. The men looked fearful…

"Relax, men! It should slow and stop as the tower is drained."

It took a very strong man to slowly lift the hatch against the weight of water still trapped in the tower, but as he slowly lifted it, the flow slowed and finally became just a dripping.

Berger was the first to go carefully up the ladder. The interior of the conning tower was a mess—twisted steel and destruction everywhere. Alarmingly, Berger could see the early morning sunlight through the large hole where the shell had entered. His next intention was to climb to the topside bridge—but the ladder had been blown away. He could see the hatch above his head—and he noted it was twisted and, he guessed, probably jammed.

Well, Berger, you can't run the boat from down here! Figure a way to climb up there and open that hatch!

He found that by climbing carefully upward using various damaged protrusions and broken brackets, he could precariously climb to within reach of the upper hatch. He reached out and attempted to turn the hatch wheel. He was not surprised when it would not turn. He was surprised, however, when he made a forlorn push upward on it—and it clanged open!

Berger scrambled up and onto the deck of the topside bridge. He quickly scanned the sea around them and he was relieved to find it empty—U-115 was by herself, at least for the moment. The deck was buckled from the explosion beneath it—he then looked upward to inspect the periscopes and found—nothing. The scopes and antennas had been wiped completely off the boat, leaving only a single piece of torn electrical cable slapping against the side of the tower.

Well, we won't need to worry about contacting headquarters! Of course, this also means we cannot call for help. Hmm…

He inspected the aft portion of the bridge and again found—nothing. The aft antiaircraft gun was gone as though it had never been there. There were other holes in the aft section of the tower, and he could now see that their port fuel blister was holed and fuel was flooding out.

Well, Berger my boy, this boat is in bad shape! I guess I'd better get us headed for home!

He yelled down to the control room and reported what he had found. He then added:

"Navigator, plot a course to the nearest submarine base—forget about France—just get us headed to the nearest base!"

Berger noted they were still headed northward, but he decided to wait to change course until he heard from the navigator.

It soon turned out that France WAS the nearest solution, so U-115 turned around and headed in that direction.

Berger then summoned two lookouts to come up, and he yelled orders down to the control room for speed and course. U-115 would have a long and slow journey on the surface to get back to friendly faces and help. There was no sign of the other boats of the wolfpack.

Thursday
March 11, 1943
08:00
USS Woodside (DD-203)

Ed awoke to the peaceful sight of a patch of sunlight dancing across the bulkhead opposite his porthole. He gingerly touched the bandage on his neck...*ouch!*

As lay there trying to fully wake up, he thought about the recent events and he realized there were big gaps in his memories. He decided to go to the wardroom and see whom, if anyone, might still be there. He walked slowly into the room and was mildly surprised to see most of his officers.

He smiled: "Well, what are all of you doing here at this fine hour of the morning?"

Bill Bevins smiled in return: "Well, Captain, we sort of expected you sometime about now."

Ed sat with relief: "Well, men, tell me what I missed."

Bevins outlined the major events and then turned to George Radcliff to supply the details. Ed smiled:

"Mr. Radcliff, I am well aware of the fine job you did fighting this ship—thank you for a great job!"

Prof smiled: "Thank you, sir. Uh, sir, how are you feeling?"

Ed touched his bandage: "Well, considering how close this was to doing me in, I'm fine. Doc tells me it's just a deep cut. He said he poured in some new stuff called 'sulfa' that's supposed to prevent infection. He taped the wound shut and here I am."

Ed continued more seriously:

"What is our current status?"

Bevins replied: "Captain, the ship and crew are fully functional. We have replaced the injured gunners. We still have several reloads available for the hedgehog, we have plenty of depth charges, and ammunition stocks are moderate. We can still fight."

"And where are we now?"

"We're about fifty miles ahead of the convoy, still headed for Liverpool."

"Do we know anything about the U-boats we attacked? Did we destroy any?"

"We have no information other than we know we hit them hard."

Ed nodded in satisfaction. He paused thoughtfully for a moment, then:

"Men, there are still a bunch of those wolves out there and it's our job to destroy them. Let's get back to an aggressive patrol! Radcliff, do we know where the subs are?"

Prof thought carefully before answering:

"Sir, the messages we have received from the British indicate there is another cluster—a 'wolfpack'—located about 300 miles east of us."

Ed looked at his Engineering Officer:

"Mr. Adams, how are we doing on fuel?"

Adams looked concerned: "Captain, we're getting a bit low—all of that steaming at flank speed burned up a lot of oil. I know we've been going a lot slower since the attacks, but it would be a good idea if we more-or-less headed towards either Reykjavik or Liverpool, whichever is closer."

"OK. Mr. Bascom, plot us a course towards the closest port that will take us near the U-boats the Brits are reporting."

It turned out they were about equidistant from Reykjavik or Liverpool, but because the convoy was bound for Liverpool, Ed decided to make Liverpool their destination. He then headed for sickbay to visit his injured crewmen.

Saturday
March 13, 1943
U-115

Berger was not entirely surprised when Kapitanleutnant Folger came slowly up through the hatch onto the bridge:

"Ach—Berger! What is our status?"

Berger described the many problems affecting U-115 and then he reported that they were on course to the nearest submarine base in Brest, France. He reported they were traveling at 10 knots and expected to reach port in approximately four more days. Folger was—not surprisingly—unhappy:

"Berger—this is terrible! We cannot simply stop fighting!"

Berger grimaced.

"Direct the boat to the shipping lanes to England and we still sink one or two on our way home."

Berger was dismayed:

"Kapitan, that is not possible! We cannot submerge, we can barely maneuver, we are low on fuel, we have only the forward deck gun to protect us from attack, and we have no way to communicate or call for assistance. I'm sorry, sir, but we will be lucky if we make it to France without being attacked by aircraft or by heavily armed and highly maneuverable surface craft."

Folger scowled:

"I am not happy to go to Brest—we must at least return to our own base at St. Nazaire. I will not drag our failure before the strangers in all of those other squadrons—I will not be laughed at!"

Berger shook his head in amazement:

"Kapitan, we cannot hope to reach St. Nazaire—we will be lucky to reach Brest! And our condition is not a 'failure'! We damaged that destroyer! And do not forget we lost four good men from the aft gun—they died fighting for the Fatherland! That is not a failure!"

Folger moved to the corner of the bridge and sulked.

*   *   *   *   *   *   *   *

Saturday crawled by at what seemed a snail's pace, but the good news was, U-115 seemed to have the ocean to herself. Sunday was much the same until late afternoon when a lookout reported smoke on the western horizon. Berger couldn't tell if it was from a steamship sailing alone, or from a damaged ship. It was at least 15 miles away, though, and of no immediate concern to the ailing U-boat. On Monday, things got interesting—in a hurry!

Berger had remained on the bridge for virtually the entire voyage towards home and he was tired. Folger came and went, but was of no practical value. Berger had met with the navigator and he was aware that they were now in their most dangerous position— limping slowly across the busy lanes approaching Scotland and England. Not only was there danger of meeting enemy warships, but they were now beneath the canopy of enemy airplane patrols. Berger was very nervous.

At 09:14, Berger's worst fear was realized—a patrolling Liberator bomber droned over in the distance and it obviously sighted U-115. Berger ordered the deck gun manned and the boat to be buttoned up. He watched the airplane carefully—if attacked, he could steer by giving rudder commands, but he wasn't confident the response would be fast enough to dodge enemy bombs.

As he feared, the bomber turned and approached from U-115's stern. Normally, his gunners would have had a great opportunity to bring down the intruder but, now, with no aft-facing anti-aircraft gun, the boat was defenseless.

The big, four-engined bomber lumbered closer. As it neared, Berger realized it had seen the damaged submarine had no rear-facing gunnery. The bomber continued remorselessly and its nose gunner began firing a fusillade at the submarine. At what the bomb aimer felt was the right moment, two large bombs fell away from the airplane and hurtled toward U-115.

"Full left rudder!" Berger yelled the command into the mouthpiece of the bridge communicator.

The boat began its turn and, to Berger's relief, both bombs fell harmlessly behind and to starboard.

At that moment, the bomber made a crucial mistake. It continued straight on its course—which, as it passed over the boat, brought it within range of Berger's deck gun:

"Deck gun—open fire!"

The gun barked and a blossom of smoke exploded just behind the bomber. Within seconds, another sharp crack and yet another blossom of smoke, this time appearing just beneath the airplane, which banked suddenly to the right and curved away. One final shot and the bomber left.

Berger knew they had been lucky. He also knew the airplane had most certainly radioed the position of U-115 and that other searchers would soon be on his trail. Berger brought the boat back on course.

Just moments later he was surprised about out of his skin— about 500 yards off to starboard rose a familiar shape from the depths: another U-boat surfaced nearby and quickly matched U-115's course and speed! The Kapitan of that boat called in his loud hailer:

"Ahoy U-boat! Is your radio out of commission?"

Berger nodded vigorously and pointed to the bare top of the conning tower. He fumbled around to find their hailer and then briefly explained what had happened.

The other boat responded:

"We will radio Brest and tell them you are coming. I will also demand they send a Schnellboot boat to escort you and protect you from the big birds."

Berger expressed his thanks. The other boat remained on station for nearly an hour before bidding Berger goodbye and quietly submerging. Berger suddenly felt very lonely.

At just past noon, the lookout called:

"Sir, I hear a powerful boat coming from ahead of us—I cannot see it yet!"

Berger was about to order U-115 turned to face the oncoming threat when, with obvious joy, the lookout called again:

"Sir! It's a Schnellboot! It's one of us!"

Sure enough, the powerful boat—called by the British an "E-boat" (meaning "enemy boat")—snarled alongside U-115. Another loud-hailer conversation occurred:

Berger: "I am happy to see you!"

S-boat: "It looks like you took a beating!"

Berger: "Yes! How did you arrive so quickly?"

S-boat: "We were patrolling northwest of Ireland in case some of the convoys tried to slip off to the south."

Berger: "We appreciate your protection. We have no communications, only our forward deck gun is serviceable, and we cannot submerge."

The S-boat commander waved and the S-boat took station about 100 yards off U-115's starboard side. Suddenly, Berger didn't feel so alone.

At ten knots, U-115 still had a long, slow journey ahead of her. Brest was still about two days away, but once they slipped past Ireland and St. George's Channel, they could hope for air cover from their German bases in France.

The afternoon passed slowly as U-115 and her escort moved southward past Ireland and toward the Scilly Isles. Berger knew sundown would be at about 19:30 and he longed for the protection of darkness. They almost made it.

At 18:15, the S-boat commander shouted across to Berger:

"Aircraft approaching! It looks like a Sunderland flying boat! We'll circle away and provide you with covering fire!"

The S-boat's engines snarled to a higher tempo and the boat lifted and began a high-speed circuit around U-115. Berger ordered the deck gun readied again.

The huge seaplane lumbered toward U-115. Berger thought to himself that such a huge and slow plane shouldn't be much of an opponent.

The airplane approached and suddenly the sea around U-115 was roiled by heavy machinegun fire. Shells were striking the boat, some piercing the thin metal outer cover and others were chewing up the wooden deck. Some struck the pressure hull and bounced off, ricocheting away. The noise was enormous, especially when the S-boat opened fire on the attacker. It was a cacophony of bullets and shells and shrieking metal, all underscored by the growling of the S-boat's powerful engines.

The airplane seemed immune to anything the S-boat could throw at it—it just droned along as it made its attack run. As it passed overhead, two bombs dropped.

"Hard right rudder!"

U-115 responded slowly, but the bombs missed. The nearest, however, fell just ten feet off the aft starboard side. The huge explosion thrust the submarine into the air and its twisting flight ended as it splashed heavily back into the sea. Berger, the lookouts, and the gunners were nearly thrown from the boat. The aircraft droned away and circled to attack again. Suddenly Berger heard an urgent call from below:

"Sir! The starboard engine has run away—I think the explosion blew off the propeller!"

Berger had no time to deal with that information—the plane approached resolutely for another attack.

Again, the froth of machinegun bullets roiling the sea and striking the boat. Again the slow and determined approach and, again, the two bombs falling from the plane.

"Hard left rudder!"

This time, U-115 managed to dodge aside and the bombs simply blew holes in the ocean.

The airplane passed overhead and, suddenly, the S-boat gunners found the range. The big seaplane started to smoke and it flew a wobbly path as it abruptly turned away and departed.

Now Berger could concentrate on the new damage. They now were powerless—the port screw was unusable and the starboard screw was probably gone. It seemed to be the end of U-115.

The S-boat came back alongside and Berger hailed the commander with his latest news. Berger fully expected the commander to recommend they take the submarine's crew aboard the S-boat and let U-115 sink to her final resting place. However, to Berger's puzzlement, the S-boat speeded up and pulled in front of the disabled sub.

"Grab this line and make it fast—we'll tow you! Hurry!"

The S-boat commander later explained that it was vital that they somehow speed up before the Royal Navy sent a destroyer or two. He felt that his powerful boat could tow the U-115 at close to 20 knots and get them to safety much more quickly.

When the towline was securely attached, the boat slowly pulled ahead to take up the slack in the line, then he gently advanced the throttles on his three powerful engines. The S-boat dug its stern into the sea and the U-boat began to move. The 6000 horsepower diesels had no trouble pulling the wallowing load at an ever-increasing speed. Towing that fast wasn't usually recommended, but it was the best option under the circumstances. The unusual duo was passing the Scilly Isles as darkness finally settled.

Through that dark night, Berger stayed topside and he was amazed—it felt as if they were simply skimming across the sea! The speed they were moving was faster than he had ever traveled in a U-boat and the tow was proceeding smoothly. At dawn, Berger began to see, far ahead, the shadowed profile of land—it was Brittany!

U-115 was towed into the Brest submarine base at 13:00 hours. Base personnel and other U-boat crews paused in their labors to watch the beat-up and helpless submarine pass on its way into one of the covered sub pens. U-115 was safe and she would fight again. Berger and the crew of U-115 had much to be grateful for to the commander and crew of S-103.

Saturday
March 13, 1943
USS Woodside (DD-203)
56.75° N X 25.50° W

Ed was back in command and *Woodside* was on her way to engage the enemy. On Saturday morning, as he sat in his Captain's chair on the bridge, he was reflecting upon a very disturbing series of messages they had received early Friday morning. As *Woodside* was barging into the submarine wolfpack and attacking five U-boats single-handedly, momentous events were occurring miles behind them at convoy HX-228. *Woodside* intercepted messages that the convoy had been attacked by several U-boats, and they could not have been the boats *Woodside* attacked. Obviously, another wolfpack had slipped in after *Woodside* passed and they were very effective: six ships had been sunk and one was damaged. The group *Woodside* attacked was apparently the next wolfpack up the line.

Ed pondered the news—it struck him as noteworthy that the attacks had come AFTER *Bogue* and her group had departed and AFTER *Woodside* had raced ahead of the convoy. How did the Germans time their attack so perfectly? Luck? A message leaked by a spy? Could the Germans be intercepting Allied radio transmissions? Had they placed a scouting boat to observe the convoy?

Ed was chagrined.

He was very aware that his ship was nearing the location the British had indicated as harboring another wolfpack. The latest word was that there were 126 U-boats at sea and many of them were clustered right where *Woodside* and HX-228 were headed. He was especially upset that the whole hunter-killer concept had been thrown away just as they might have made a significant difference. Obviously, the U-boat the airplane tried—and failed—to attack was one of the pack that later nailed the convoy. The carrier planes and destroyers were supposed to be working together but that hadn't happened. Worse yet, to Ed's mind, was the fact that the carrier had stuck right along with the convoy instead of ranging ahead aggressively. It was very exasperating.

LTJG Radcliff stepped out of the Ops Center and approached Ed:

"Captain, I'm sorry to interrupt you, but we just received a very detailed message from Liverpool regarding the locations of the U-boats in this area. We've plotted the eighteen—eighteen!—nearest ones. Most are to the south of us, but there is one right ahead and two directly beyond it. There are also two further north."

Ed rushed to view the plot board.

"Prof, what are the distances we're talking about?"

"Sir, the nearest one is about 20 miles ahead. The next closest is directly east of him by about 60 miles. This third one is directly in line east of that by about 50 miles."

"If we designate these three in a line as number 1, 2, and 3, let's call the nearest one north as #4 and the farthest north as #5. It looks like #5 is too far away…"

Prof nodded: "Yes sir—it's about 150 miles away."

"…and #4 is out of our way, too."

"Yes, about 85 miles away."

"But if we steam straight through #1, #2, and 3#, we can just plow right through—and they're far enough apart for us to rearm before we reach the next one in line."

Prof nodded.

"Navigator—what's our course to intercept #1 and then carry through along the line?"

LT. Bascom did a quick plot:

"Course to number 1 is 010 degrees true."

"Coxswain—come to 010 true."

Suddenly, Griffin Stone called out:

"Plot—Radar: I have a contact, range 35000 yards, bearing 045 degrees relative!"

Soon, *Woodside* rang with the strident command "General Quarters! General Quarters! All hands man your battle stations!" This was followed by the pounding of feet as the men raced for their assigned stations. All the while, Ed was pondering carefully…

"Radar—how far to contact #1?"

Stone looked carefully:

"Range is now 31000 yards."

"Radio: notify the convoy that we are attacking a line of three U-boats at 56.51°W X 25.51°N. There are two additional enemy located north of our position including one at about 58° N X 22° W. I recommend the convoy detour north to at least 65°N."

LTJG Radcliff turned to the Captain:

"Captain, is there any way we could get airplanes out here to help?"

"Good question, Prof. Radio—try to contact the convoy center in Liverpool and report what we've found. Ask if there are any aircraft available to assist in an attack."

Ed decided not to rush things;

"Engine room—turns for 8 knots, please."

Radcliff looked questioningly at him:

"Prof, if we attack, I'll take us down the line again, engaging each boat as we encounter it. But, first, I want to get a clearer picture of the situation—and I want to hear from Liverpool. We'll just stooge around out here for a while."

In the radio room, Phil Summers was a busy man—transmitting and receiving at a furious pace. He appreciated that Pete Perkins noticed how stressed he was and moved in to help. Between them, the vital communications went out and—eventually—answers were received.

"Bridge—Radio: The convoy confirms receipt of our message."

About five minutes later:

"Bridge—Radio: Liverpool says there is one aircraft in our vicinity—a Liberator at the far edge of its patrol. The plane is armed and can assist in an attack. They have been ordered to rendezvous with us at this location. They are expected to meet us in about ten minutes."

"OK, thanks!

Ed began scanning the sky. He had a thought:

"Radio—will we be able to talk to the airplane?"

Summers smiled:

"Captain, I requested the frequency for the airplane, and—yes—we should be able to talk to them."

"Voice or key?"

'It will be by key or flashing light, sir."

"Good, get the signalman up here right away."

"Plot—Radar: I have an incoming aircraft bearing 105 degrees, distance 10000 yards."

The minutes passed quickly and soon, one of the lookouts reported:

"Sir, I hear an airplane bearing about 100 degrees true."

In moments the huge bomber swooped over *Woodside* and began to circle the ship. Communication was established and a plan was hatched as a way to attack the enemy boats. It was decided that when *Woodside* closed to 6000 yards, the airplane would make a diving attack on the U-boat selected as the first target. If the plane's attack didn't sink the sub or, if the sub submerged, *Woodside* would race to the target and attack with the hedgehog and depth charges. Both *Woodside* and the airplane would then continue to the next sub in line and repeat the process, and then onward to do the same for contact #3. Both ship and airplane shared the same overriding problem, however—fuel. Both were near their limits and needed to head for home. It was far from a perfect plan, but with just one destroyer and one airplane, it was the best they could do.

Ed began to shout orders:

"All ahead full! Guns, prepare to fire on my order! Torpedo— await my order! Hedgehog—get ready!"

"Plot—radar: target bears 000 degrees, distance 28000 yards."

The ship raced ahead…

"Distance to target 26000 yards."

And so went Stoney's litany of reports. The minutes passed and everyone was filled with anticipation.

The lookouts on the U-boat had seen the circling airplane and were puzzled by why it was circling. From their position low on the water, they could not yet see the oncoming destroyer. The U-boat commander was confident his gunners could take care of the bomber if it attacked. He chose to remain on the surface and fight the airplane.

"Distance to target 12000 yards."

Ed had the phone talker check to make sure every station was fully manned and ready. He was a bit uneasy about attacking a surfaced U-boat in broad daylight, but having the airplane helped.

It took about 15 minutes more to reach the key 6000-yard mark.

"Distance 6000 yards!"

"Report to the airplane!"

Ed's order was no more out of his mouth than the big bird roared overhead and went after the sub.

In addition to the airplane, the U-boat lookouts had just seen the destroyer racing in their direction. The commander still wasn't worried—he could knock down the airplane and then engage the destroyer. He was calm as the airplane started its approach.

Woodside sped toward the submarine, but all eyes were on the airplane. The bomber quickly closed the distance—the U-boat opened fire with its anti-aircraft guns and the plane fired its nose-mounted machine guns at the sub. The plane reached its drop point and, from an altitude of about 300 feet, dropped two 250-pound depth charges which closely straddled the sub. The men on *Woodside's* bridge eagerly watched to see what would happen.

The depth charges exploded just beside and slightly beneath the rear of the sub and the sea erupted and carried the sub upward with it. Pitched severely into the air, the U-boat crewmen held on to avoid being thrown into the ocean. When the boat came back down, they quickly scrambled to regain their fighting positions. Ed watched as the sub settled back to an even keel:

"All guns that can bear—open fire!"

The German commander thought he saw the airplane circling for another attack and he saw the onrushing destroyer firing at him and he decided that discretion might be a good idea.

"Submerge! Crash dive!"

Ed saw the boat tilt and start downward—he knew it was submerging and he was ready for his hedgehog attack. But then something stunned him—the sub began its dive and angled down at a normal angle for submerging when, suddenly, the bow dropped and the stern rose sharply to the sky and the sub sliced quickly beneath the surface pointing almost straight down. Apparently, the plane had damaged the boat and when it started to submerge, it suddenly flooded and was now out of control and heading for the bottom!

"Plot—Sonar: I hear sounds of the submarine flooding. There's a lot of racket going on inside it!"

As much as Ed wanted to stick around to be sure the sub sank, he knew they had to hurry on to the next boat. The airplane had not been circling to attack—it was merely getting in position to go after the next boat down the line, some 60 miles away.

"Sonar—do you think it's sinking?"

Wirtz had been listening carefully:

"Captain, based on what I'm hearing, I think it's sinking."

Ed smiled:

"Radio—send to the plane 'Score one for you!'"

At her current speed of thirty knots, it would take *Woodside* over two hours to cover the sixty miles to the next boat. The bomber returned to circling the destroyer as it hurried eastward. Either the next U-boat had received a radio transmission from the first boat, or had simply heard the explosions, but that commander wasn't taking any chances:

"Dive! Dive! Take her down!"

As *Woodside* approached the location of the second submarine, the airplane signaled that it had lost contact.

"Plot—Sonar: I have a submerged submarine bearing 358 degrees, distance 5000 yards. It's moving northward at about 4 knots."

Ed smiled—this one was their turn!

"Radio—notify the plane that we have the sub on sonar and we are attacking."

"Sonar—guide us to the sub. Hedgehog and depth charges—be ready. Set depth charges for medium depth."

"Captain," Wirtz said, "I could hear a lot better if we'd slow down a little."

"Engine room—make turns for 12 knots."

Wirtz reported as the range closed until they were at the point to fire the hedgehog. Pop—Pop—Pop, the projectiles fired and the familiar splashes appeared ahead. Everyone waited breathlessly for the boom! of a successful strike—they were rewarded with one hit.

"Roll depth charges! All ahead full!"

The usual fountains of water blasted skyward. *Woodside* circled away to allow the noise to subside. Finally, Wirtz reported:

"Plot—Sonar: there's a lot of noise from the sub, but it still seems to be under control. I think we hurt it badly—but it doesn't seem to be sinking."

"Roger."

The signalman spoke:

"Captain, we just got a blinker signal from the airplane that they getting critically low on fuel. They will go on ahead and attack the third sub and then continue on home."

"OK. Tell them: 'Thanks—and good hunting!'"

Lieutenant Adams called from the engine room and reported that fuel was becoming a serious consideration for *Woodside.* Ed told him they were headed for Liverpool, but there was one more sub in the way along their route.

By the time *Woodside* arrived at the reported location of the third U-boat, the surface was empty and radar reported nothing nearby. However…

"Plot—Sonar: submerged contact bearing 350 degrees, distance 4500 yards. Apparently, the plane drove it under."

Ed responded:

"Prepare to attack submerged U-boat! Helm—come left as directed by sonar."

"Plot: target bears distance now 4000 yards, helm, come left ten degrees."

Soon;

"Plot: target bears 000 degrees, distance 2500 yards."

Ed called:

"Hedgehog, prepare to attack!"

"Maintain present heading, distance 1500 yards." A pause, then: "Captain, he just turned and we're coming up behind him!"

Suddenly the port lookout screamed: "Torpedo approaching from the port bow!"

Simultaneously, Wirtz yelled:

"High-speed screws! Torpedo in the water bearing 000 degrees and closing fast!"

Ed decided that if the torpedo was approaching from dead ahead, he'd be better off to comb its wake by remaining pointed directly at the sub. He watched out the bridge windows and picked up the trail of bubbles from the incoming missile. It looked like it was coming at a very slight angle towards the port bow.

"Helm—10 degrees left rudder! There—steady as you go!"

The torpedo would now stream along the port side and should clear the ship. Unfortunately, turbulence caused by *Woodside's* quick jog caught the torpedo and pulled it in, causing it to sideswipe the after hull. There was a tremendous explosion and *Woodside* shook like a dog shaking a cotton doll.

"Get me a damage report! Helm—can you still steer?"

"Yes, sir, but it doesn't respond very well."

"Sonar, where is the target?"

"Target bears 005 degrees, 800 yards."

"Helm—five degrees right rudder!"

"Target is 250 yards!"

"Hedgehog—fire! Depth charges—Ed counted the seconds needed to pass over the target—roll depth charges!"

"Where's my damage report?"

Everything seemed to happen at once—the hedgehog charges brought two explosions and the depth charges brought the usual mayhem astern. During all of this, the damage report came in:

"Sir, damage control reports no visible breaches in the hull. The men in after steering are not responding to calls. The engine room reports they have shut down the port shaft—it must be damaged. No other personnel casualties reported yet."

"Helm—do you still have control?"

"Uh—sort of."

"What! What does that mean?"

"Well, as I turn the helm for a starboard turn to clear the area, we aren't turning like we should. We're turning, but not very well."

The phone talker reported:

"Sir—more damage reports: two of the depth charge crew were injured when the explosion slammed them into the port rack. The other men are OK. The 40 MM gun and crew are unharmed. The aft peak tank seems to be leaking."

Ed knew the peak tank was filled with fresh water and he wasn't concerned about that. The apparent steering and port screw damage were much more concerning.

As he was considering all this, Wirtz reported:

"Plot—Sonar: I hear breaking up noises—I think we got the sub!"

"Radar—are there any other targets out there?"

"No, Captain, my screen is clear out to 40000 yards in all directions."

"Sonar—any other targets?"

"No, sir—I can hear the sub breaking up, but my screen is empty."

Ed then called the engine room and spoke with Lieutenant Adams:

"Mr. Adams—what is our status?"

"Sir, the starboard engine and screw seem fine. The port screw or shaft is damaged and not usable."

"Any people injured down there?"

"No, sir—we got shook really bad, but we're all OK."

"How fast can we go?"

"Captain, balancing speed with fuel consumption, I'd recommend we not exceed 12 knots."

"Roger. Thanks."

"Navigator, what's our course to Liverpool?"

Bascom did another quick plot:

"Course to the North Channel is 095 degrees, 550 miles. At 12 knots, we'll enter the channel in two days."

"Make it so."

Monday
March 15, 1943
USS Woodside (DD-203)

It was just after dawn on Monday, March 15 when *Woodside* curved around Northern Ireland, passed Rathlin Island to starboard, and headed for the Isle of Man and on toward Liverpool. During the journey, they encountered no other U-boats, but the men of *Woodside* had been very busy nonetheless.

One major issue was the fate of the seven men stationed in the after steering compartment when the torpedo hit. Immediately after the explosion, the port rear damage control party approached the hatch leading below hoping it wasn't jammed shut. To their relief, it opened normally. No smoke issued forth, and they saw no flooding, so two of the men climbed down, expecting the worst. Upon reaching the cramped room, they saw seven bodies sprawled on the deck. As they approached the first body, they were startled when the man slowly opened his eyes and groggily asked "What happened?" The other bodies began to shift position and slowly, all seven men regained consciousness. There was great relief that the men were unharmed, although they would suffer from headaches for a couple of days. The damage control men explained about the torpedo that hit the hull just outside their location. After a few minutes, the men had recovered sufficiently to carefully inspect their surroundings. The first thing they saw was that the hull on the port side was dished in by nearly a foot. They also soon found that the hydraulic steering ram had been displaced from its mount and the rudder was not able to swing smoothly—which accounted for the difficulty in steering experienced on the bridge

The damage control party continued their evaluation from topside and found that the peak tank wasn't leaking after all—the water that had been seen was actually seawater running off following the explosion. Careful examination indicated no sprung seams or hull leaks. Any damage below the water was, of course, invisible to them.

Once *Woodside* was well on her way, a repair party returned to after steering and worked to restore the hydraulic equipment to its proper position. At one point, it was necessary to stop *Woodside* while the repairman disconnected the ram, repositioned it, and remounted it properly. Then they reconnected the rudder and *Woodside* got underway again. Steering still wasn't quite right, but it was much better than earlier.

As they steamed along, Ed sent reports to Atlantic Fleet headquarters and to the Royal Navy folks in Liverpool. He asked Liverpool if *Woodside* could get some drydock time to investigate the propulsion problems. He hadn't received a direct answer— instead, he was simply ordered to come to Liverpool and moor as directed upon arrival.

It was well after dark on the 15th when *Woodside* crept slowly alongside Canada Dock and tied up.

The next morning, Ed received a summons to report to Derby House. It was like old times as he walked the streets to reach the blocky gray building. He was escorted down to the Western

Approaches Command headquarters where he was introduced to Lieutenant Commander Finch.

Finch didn't waste any time:

"Commander Palmer, as you well know, time in graving dock is nearly impossible to obtain due to the numerous repairs required by our vessels. I have been made aware, however, that you have an unusual relationship here and so I have been able to get you some time in the Canada Graving Dock as soon as the cruiser that is presently there is released. I anticipate that will be sometime later this week. You will have only a short stay to identify any issues directly affecting your ship's seaworthiness. Emergency repairs will be done only to the degree to make your ship safe. Any other repairs will have to be done afloat while tied to Canada Dock or when you return to the United States."

Ed didn't appreciate the officious tone but controlled himself. He asked:

"What is the status of HX-228?"

"Other than the ships lost on the 10th, the convoy arrived safely yesterday."

"You're welcome."

Finch's head snapped up:

"What?"

"I said 'You're welcome'. A large number of U-boats were waiting for that convoy to steam right into them and they would have decimated it. Instead, my ship attacked them—an enemy in vastly superior numbers—and my ship directed the convoy to alter to a safe course. One of your aircraft was very helpful and actually sank a sub—my ship damaged another one and sank a third. That convoy, bearing food, arms, and machinery for your country made it safely through. As I said—'You're welcome'."

Finch looked angry:

"That's preposterous! The escorts reported nothing of the kind!"

"The escorts never left the convoy—we were many miles ahead of them, all alone."

"Come with me!"

Finch led Ed through the rabbit warren of hallways until they reached an office marked "Commanding Officer". Ed had enjoyed a warm relationship with the previous commander, Admiral Percy, but he hadn't met the current leader.

They were invited in and Ed was introduced to Admiral Max Horton:

"Commander Palmer, we meet at last!" Horton stood and offered his hand. "Admiral Percy spoke highly of you. From what I've just learned about your recent escapades, his regard was well-earned."

Finch seemed confused by it all.

The visitors were offered a seat and Horton continued:

"According to our sources, you and our liberator bomber attacked three U-boats: the first was sunk by the aircraft, the second was damaged by you and the aircraft, and we have confirmation that the third was confirmed as sunk by you. Good show!"

"Thank you, sir."

"You were also busy on the 11th—your ship single-handedly attacked a line of five surfaced U-boats that threatened HX-228. You might like to know the results of your pugnacity: two of these U-boats were slightly damaged but they had to leave the area temporarily to effect repairs, two others were more seriously damaged and aborted their patrols and returned to base. The fifth boat was originally reported as sunk, but it later showed up at Brest under tow by an E-boat. Apparently, it was quite a mess. Your efforts were instrumental in preventing further attacks on HX-228."

Ed smiled:

"Thank you, sir. My men will be happy to learn the news."

Then Horton asked a question Ed didn't expect:

"Commander, what are your thoughts regarding the 'hunter-killer' concept?"

That got Ed started and we went on at length describing the potential for success. He also bemoaned the failure to capitalize on the abilities of the group. He ended by saying:

"Admiral, my ship and your airplane—one ship and one airplane—had great success working together—and we'd never even heard of each other before they flew over and joined us. If one ship and one plane can be successful, imagine the potential for a fully coordinated group!"

 Horton nodded.

The meeting came to an end and Ed and Finch departed. Finch was much more cooperative.

*   *   *   *   *   *   *

When Ed returned to the ship he announced that they would remain at pier-side for a few days and he granted generous liberty. Mike Torelli was the first man off the ship after a brief stop by Joey's locker:

"Joey, the Liver Building is the one with the birds on top—right?"

"Yeah, I think so. You going to find April?"

"Uh, huh!" So saying, Mike was off the ship and on his way early Tuesday morning. He couldn't miss the huge building "with the birds on top" and he entered, excited to see April after so long apart. As he passed through the huge doors into the entry hall, he stopped—stunned by the hugeness and beauty that surrounded him. He finally composed himself and approached the information desk in the center ahead of him. A young woman smiled at him:

"Hello. May I help you?"

Mike stammered:

"Well, uh, um, I guess so…"

91

She smiled understandingly:

"It's a bit overwhelming, is it not?"

Mike nodded.

"How may I help you?"

Mike composed himself:

"I'm looking for a girl…"

The young lady looked startled and Mike noticed it:

"Oh! No, no—not that! I mean a girl I know who works here and I want to find her."

The young lady relaxed:

"Oh. For whom does she work?"

"Uhh—I don't know. I just know she works in an office here."

"Sir, there are probably a thousand people at work here! What else can you tell me?"

"Her name is April Carmody and she's about—this—tall (motioning with his hands), and her hair is sort of brown, and…"

"Sir! Wait! I'll try looking in the personnel directory, but it isn't kept up very well, so I am not hopeful."

As she scanned the bulky list, people were coming and going through the busy lobby. Suddenly, Mike heard a familiar voice.

He looked across the huge room and there, waiting to board an elevator, was April!

"Wait! There she is! April! Hey, April! April!" He started running toward the elevator. To his good fortune, the car that had just arrived was crammed with passengers and it took them a few moments to leave the elevator.

"April! Hey, April!"

April heard her name, but she couldn't imagine anyone shouting for her that way—she figured it must be for someone else. But the shouting continued, so she turned to look—

"Oh—it can't be! It can't be you! Mike! Mike—I'm here!"

Despite the crowd of people, April rushed into Mike's arms and they kissed. Some of the people seemed offended, but others clapped and one man even cheered.

Mike found April and he suddenly felt complete.

*　*　*　*　*　*　*

Early Thursday morning, a yard workman appeared on *Woodside's* quarterdeck and announced they would now be moving the ship into the drydock. Ed wanted to caution the men placing the keel blocks to be careful of the sonar head, but he need not have worried—they quite obviously knew what they were doing. The ship was towed away from the pier and nudged into the flooded drydock until positioned perfectly. The rear gate was closed and the water began to recede as the huge pumps ran. *Woodside* settled gently onto the blocks and the dock was finally empty of water. Ed couldn't wait to go into the bottom of the dock and see what damage his ship had experienced.

"Here, sir—wait!" One of the yard workers stopped Ed. "Sir, you'll need some galoshes to walk around down there."

Ed looked down and realized that, although the dock had been pumped out, there was still a fair bit of dirty water sloshing around.

"Oh. Thanks—I'll have to find some."

The man grinned: "I thought maybe you'd need some—here..."

He held out a pair of stout water-resistant galoshes. Ed tried them on and they slipped right over his regular shoes.

"Say, these are perfect—thanks!"

The yard man turned out to be the supervisor and he and Ed went aft to view the damage. They gazed at the dented and explosion-blackened plates.

"Well, sir, you were lucky! I'm guessing the torpedo hit at an angle?"

Ed nodded: "Yes, I thought it would miss along the side, but turbulence at the rear pulled it into the ship. I was guessing it was a glancing blow that was just enough to set it off."

"Yes. It appears the explosion was deflected by the ship and the force went mostly into the sea. Did it push you sideways?"

"Yes—violently."

"Well, you were very lucky—if that torpedo had hit at more of a right angle, you'd probably still be out there swimming!"

Ed winced.

The foreman continued:

"Admiral Horton, himself, directed that we do all possible to help you. Unfortunately, though, we can't replace these damaged plates—that will have to wait until you return to the U.S. Let's see what else happened…"

Ed told him about the damaged port screw or shaft. They moved to investigate and immediately saw the problem:

The foreman exclaimed: "Well, that's quite a sight!'

Ed could see the port screw had been badly bent by the explosion—the bent blades looked almost like a flower. He looked at the foreman:

The man shook his head:

"Sorry, sir, but we don't happen to have a screw with the proper diameter and blade pitch to replace this one. Obviously, this one won't function, and your shaft might be bent, too. You'll certainly be heading home on one screw." He was thoughtful for a moment:

"You know, since you'll be traveling on one screw, this mess will just cause a lot of resistance and impede your progress. We could remove this bad screw and leave it off, thereby removing all of that extra drag—but that would leave your shaft-end exposed to the sea and it could be damaged by corrosion." He thought for another moment: "But maybe we could cut off the blades—that would reduce the resistance, but still keep the prop boss in place to protect the shaft. What do you think?"

Ed smiled: "I think that's genius! Let's do it!"

Next, they scrutinized the rudder:

Ed described the issues with steering they had experienced and the worker looked carefully at the huge rudder:

"Hmm. I can't really tell without careful measurement, but it seems a little out of kilter. Maybe the explosion bent the rudder or the rudder post. Were you able to steer the ship after they fixed the hydraulics?"

"Yes—we managed. It wasn't quite right, but we had firm control."

The man shook his head:

"Well, Captain, it seems like there's not much here we can do to help you. Other than replacing your bridge windows, your hull plates aren't leaking, the rudder works—mostly, and the bent screw is about all we can help with. I'll get a crew here right away to cut away those prop blades and then we'll float you back out."

"That'll be fine—thanks!"

As they were finishing their investigation, Mr. Adams, the Engineering Officer arrived, so Ed quickly explained to him what they had found and the plan to address it. Adams just shook his head and began planning how to steam more than 3000 miles home on only their starboard screw.

* * * * * * * *

Mike and April spent every possible minute together. Much of her day was taken by her work in an office that tracked the quantity of foodstuffs imported for Liverpool's use. Orders were placed to maintain required levels of stocks, and April's clerical skills assisted in maintaining the huge volume of paperwork that was generated. When they were together, however, it was as though they hadn't been apart. They talked seriously about their future and both agreed that marriage was the goal. Mike knew there was still a lot of war ahead and his job on a destroyer was extremely hazardous. He had heard something about sailors being offered life insurance that could go to their wife or family, but he didn't really know anything about it.

On Wednesday morning, while the ship was still waiting to go into drydock, Mike stopped by the ship's office and asked the yeoman about the insurance:

"Yes, you are entitled to up to a $10,000 life insurance policy. There is no cost to you. Your beneficiary can be your wife or family."

"Can I sign it to a girlfriend?"

The man smiled: "No—sorry. You have to be married. There are too many girls out there who just want the money and they cheat the men to get it"

97

"Oh. Well, thanks!"

Mike gave the matter a lot of thought and decided he'd find out if he and April could get married now.

The two lovers met during April's lunch break to discuss the idea:

"April, are you sure you want to marry me?"

She smiled:

"Oh, yes! I've wanted us to get married ever since you saved me!"

Mike grinned:

"Well, I think it's a good idea, too. But how do we do it?"

April thought carefully:

"I think am still considered a member of our parish in Anfield— maybe the Rector will accept that and he will marry us. If you go to Anfield, go to St. Margaret, not St. Columba."

"I'll go out there and try to ask him. I'll see you tonight. Bye!"

Mike was becoming rather adept at figuring out the Liverpool bus system and, an hour later, was standing on the corner of Belmont Road and Rocky Lane, looking up at beautiful St. Margaret church. He climbed the steps and opened the door. Inside was an ornate building that took his breath away. He remembered he should remove his cap, and then walked slowly toward the front. He was chagrined that he seemed to be all alone.

He was standing before the altar when he heard a door open somewhere out of sight and, much to his relief, an older man wearing what Mike thought of as "priest's clothes" came in from the side. The man saw Mike:

"Oh—hello there, young man. May I assist you?"

Mike was very nervous, but he explained his reason for being there. To his relief, the man smiled:

"My son, we might just be able to help you. Come with me to the office and we'll see if your young lady is one of us."

In the office, the man went to a huge book and began turning pages:

"Ah, here we are: Carmody, April Louise, born October 17, 1922. Confirmed November 3, 1930. Daughter of Hubert and Ethel Carmody. Does that sound like the right girl?"

Mike nodded eagerly: "Yes, sir!"

"And what is your religious persuasion?"

Mike pondered the question:

"Well, we always went to the Catholic church near home."

Following several more questions, the man rose and offered his hand:

"Under the circumstances, I will be happy to conduct the ceremony. I realize time is a problem these days—when would you like the event to occur?"

Mike was stumped:

"Well—uh—I don't really know. I'll have to talk to April and to my Captain. Can I let you know later?"

"Of course. Just give me as much advance warning as you can."

They shook hands again and Mike embarked on his journey back to downtown.

After April got off work Wednesday evening, they discussed their next steps:

"Mike, I need to tell my parents and you are supposed to ask my father for my hand." She giggled—then asked: "Do you want to come out to Grandmother's and do it now?"

Mike was terrified at the thought:

"Gee, April, do I really have to ask your dad? What if he says 'no'? Can't you just ask your mom or something?"

April smiled:

"Are you telling me my big, brave husband is afraid of my father?"

"Aw, April!"

In the end, Mike accepted his duty and they climbed on the bus to Sutton, arriving just in time for dinner. Mike hadn't made it all the way out there during this brief stay in Liverpool, so he hadn't seen the family for several months. They received him very warmly, though, and congratulated him on his promotion from several months ago. Mike smiled, but he was obviously very nervous.

"April," Mrs. Carmody suggested, "why don't we clear away the dishes and let Mike and your father have chat?"

Mr. Carmody sat by the fire and lit his pipe. Mike fidgeted. Mr. Carmody sensed that something was up:

"Michael, you seem nervous this evening—is there something wrong?"

Mike took a deep breath:

"No, sir—there's nothing wrong. It's just that—"

"Yes?"

"Well, you see, April and I want to get married—but I guess I have to get your permission. (Nervous pause) Will you? I mean, will you let us get married?" It all came out in a rush.

Mr. Carmody was taken aback—he knew the young people claimed to be in love, but—married? Hmmm.

"Well, Michael, that's quite something. Married, eh? You really love my daughter enough to spend the rest of your life with her?"

Mike nodded enthusiastically: "Yes, sir!"

Carmody nodded thoughtfully:

"Do you think getting married in the middle of a war is a good idea?"

Mike was worried:

"Well, yes, sir. We want to be together, and I want her to have my insurance in case anything happens. Besides, I want her to move to New York with me."

"Oh, my! That's really something!" Another pause. Then: "How will you support her in New York?"

April and Mike had discussed that:

"Well, for now, we have my Navy pay. After the war, I'll probably get a job at the shipyard—they pay real good and we could do great."

"I see." He was quietly thoughtful for a couple of minutes: "Do you mind if we ask April to join us?"

"No, sir—I'd love that!"

Not only did April join them, so did Mrs. Carmody and Grandmother.

A long discussion ensued covering all the points raised by Father, but it soon became obvious that the women of the family had already decided the marriage was a good idea. Finally, Father gave in:

"Well, Michael, it seems there is excited support for your marriage to April, so—I give you my approval and my blessing."

April rushed and wrapped her father in a huge hug.

"Oh, Da—thank you!"

The only remaining hurdle was the Navy, and Mike would have to talk to Captain Palmer in the morning.

Unfortunately, Thursday morning was the day the ship went into drydock, so Mike couldn't talk with the Captain until later. Finally, after lunch, he learned the Captain was in his cabin, so he decided to try to see him. There was one other thing, however:

"Joey—I need to go to talk to the Captain about marrying April, but I'm scared. I've never talked to the Captain of the ship before! But, hey, Joey, you talk to him all the time—will you come and help me?"

Joey smiled:

"Mike, he won't bite you—he's actually a pretty nice guy."

"Joeeeyyy?"

"OK, come on 'fraidy cat and I'll help you."

Ed was in his cabin and had just finished his mid-day meal. The drydock was flooding and *Woodside* would soon be back out and tied to Canada Dock. He was pondering what might come next when there was a knock at his door:

"Come!"

Joey opened the door and ushered Mike inside:

Joey spoke: "Hello, Captain—Donatelli, Soundman Third and Torelli, Gunner's Mate Third. May we have a word with you?"

Ed smiled to himself—the Torelli fellow looked terrified.

103

"Of course, Donatelli—what can I do for you?"

Joey urged Mike to describe his situation, which he did in rather halting tones. Mike ended by asking:

"So, Captain, I need to know what to do so the Navy will let me marry her."

Ed felt sorry for the poor frightened sailor:

"Well, Torelli, there is nothing to prevent you from marrying a foreign national, but there are some things you need to consider. First is that we don't know when—if ever—we might return to Liverpool. You might not see your wife again until the war is over. Also, we are engaged in highly hazardous duty and there is no guarantee we will even survive the war. And you need to realize that getting her to the United States will be a very long and difficult process. Have you thought of that?"

Mike nodded: "We talked all about that—but we still want to get married."

"I have one simple question—why?"

Mike was lost for a minute:

"Uh, well, because I love her and she loves me."

Joey interceded and explained that this was the girl Mike had rescued back during the May Blitz.

Ed nodded: "Ah."

"Well, Torelli, there is a pile of paperwork you'll need to complete. When did you want to have the ceremony?"

"I don't know, Captain—I guess it depends on how long we're here."

"Um—good point. At this point…"

Ed was interrupted by another knock on his door.

"Come!"

It was the quarterdeck messenger bringing a sheaf of papers that contained orders for *Woodside's* immediate future.

Ed quickly scanned the papers, then looked up at Mike and Joey:

"Torelli, you are a lucky man—these papers are our orders and I see we will remain here until departing for the United States on Saturday, March 27. It looks like you have about a week to get hitched."

"Oh, wow!" Mike couldn't contain his excitement. "I'll tell April and we'll talk to her church guy and get it scheduled. Thanks! Oops—I mean—Thanks, Sir!"

Ed laughed as the men left his cabin.

The wedding took place Tuesday morning, March 23, in front of the very altar where Mike first met the Rector. Joey Donatelli served as Mike's assistant—or "Best Man", while April was assisted by her friend Rachel from work. April's mother, father, and grandmother were present as were several of the guys who'd gone through boot camp with Mike. The fellows had taken up a collection and gave the money to Mike "so he could have a nice wedding night".

The ceremony began at 10:00 AM and by 10:20. Mike and April were officially man and wife. Both couldn't stop smiling— although April smiled through her tears of joy. The newlyweds left the church in a taxi and went to the Adelphi Hotel. It took every penny they had, but their two-day/one-night stay at the fabulous hostelry was the most astounding thing either of them had experienced in all their young lives.

* * * * * * *

While Mike and April were beginning their life together, *Woodside* had been floated out of drydock and was tied to the side of Canada Dock. Workers then come aboard and began the installation of the bridge glass. Ed's orders directed *Woodside* to depart on Saturday, March 27, and steam directly to New York for repairs at the Navy Yard. Ed huddled with Lieutenant Adams to plan the best speed for the transit so as not to overstrain their single functioning shaft and screw. He then met with LTJG Radcliff to plan their response to any intruders they might encounter, and with Lieutenant Bascom, the Navigator, to plot the best course for the journey.

"Carl," said Ed, "I'm tempted to go south from here and out through St. George's Channel—there are probably fewer U-boats down there. Although it galls me, we are not in any condition to take on another wolfpack."

Bascom nodded in agreement:

"I agree. Based on the information we have from the Convoy Center, there are only a couple of wolves down there and we should be able to avoid them."

"How long will it take us at 12 knots?"

Bascom shook his head:

"A long time—we're looking at about eleven days."

"Well, so much for being a 'Greyhound of the Sea'!"

*   *   *   *   *   *   *

Newly-married Mike Torelli returned to the ship late on Wednesday evening with stars in his eyes. His friends greeted him with grins, jokes, and slaps on the back. He fell into his rack and quickly dropped off to sleep.

Early Thursday morning, with Joey along to help, Mike went to the yeoman and signed up for the insurance. He had to present his marriage certificate and fill out a bunch of papers. When that was complete, he went to leave the office, but the yeoman stopped him:

"Torelli, are you wanting your new wife to move to the U.S.?"

Mike nodded.

"Well, you're going to have a huge amount of paperwork to complete and get approved before that can happen. Since our U.S. Embassy is all the way in London, maybe you can get started with the government people here. Your wife is going to be a very busy lady after we leave."

Mike and April quizzed several people and received suggestions regarding which government office to visit. They followed the advice and by Thursday evening had realized that April would not be sailing off to New York anytime soon.

*   *   *   *   *   *   *

Woodside slipped out of the Canada Basin and headed south and then west toward home. There were far fewer U-boats in that area, but there were U-boats.

"Plot—Radar: I have a surface contact bearing 350 degrees relative, distance 32000 yards. It is moving southeastward at about 10 knots."

Ed was nervous:

"Can you tell what it is? A U-boat? An E-boat? What?"

"I can only judge by the size of the return—I don't think it's large enough to be a ship, but maybe a patrol boat or a sub. My guess is a sub…"

Ed watched as the contact was plotted—it appeared to be a vessel headed away from Woodside's path and toward northern France.

Prof spoke up: "Sir, my guess is it's a sub returning to Brest. If we hold our course and speed, I don't think he'll even know we're here."

Ed nodded.

It turned out exactly that way, and the rest of the voyage was without excitement—it ended up being a long, slow, uncomfortable journey. Happily, they sighted the towers of New York at mid-morning, Tuesday, April 6.

*   *   *   *   *   *   *

 The ship Moored to Pier D and settled down to yet another stay in the Navy Yard. At just after 15:00, Ed was summoned to the wardroom to meet with the now-much-too-familiar Mr. Jamison from the Yard.

Ed entered the room and Jamison was standing at the sideboard with a mug of coffee in his hand. He looked at Ed with a reproachful gaze:

Ed smiled: "I know, Jamison, we forgot to duck again…"

Jamison grimaced:

"Captain, you're awfully hard on this poor old lady."

Ed just nodded. At that moment, another person entered:

"Sigsbee!" Ed was shocked: "What in the world are you doing here?"

Captain Sigsbee looked serious:

"Well, Ed, it seems like *Woodside* is either at sea attacking hordes of submarines, or propped up here being put back together. We need to talk—and I asked Mr. Jamison to join us."

Ed was concerned: *This sounds serious—I wonder what's going on…*

The men sat down and Sigsbee spoke:

"Ed, the success you've had with *Woodside* has been exceptional." He paused: "But these damages have been taking a toll on your ship. She's an old lady—what, 23 years old now? And we need to decide about the future." He turned to the yardman: "Jamison, you've read the report from Liverpool—what do you think of the repairs that are necessary?"

"Well, Captain, I won't know for sure until we get the old gal in drydock but, based on that report, she needs a new screw, possible shaft repairs, possible rudder repairs, some hull repairs, and we don't know what else."

"Do you have a screw for her?"

"Yep—we hauled one out from our surplus lot, so that's not a big problem."

"Based upon the report, is it your judgment that this ship is worth the cost, time, and effort to repair her?"

Ed caught his breath:

"Stu—you're not thinking of scrapping her?!"

Sigsbee looked at Ed with a level gaze:

"Ed, I'm getting a lot of flak from Washington about the almost continual repairs your aged ship requires."

Ed exploded:

"That's utter nonsense! This ship has not required repairs due to her age! Her repairs come from actively engaging the enemy and sustaining serious battle damage! I'll stack our accomplishments against any other ship in the fleet! This is outrageous!"

Sigsbee smiled:

"That's exactly what I told them—in nicer language, of course."

Ed continued to fume. Sigsbee continued:

"It has been recognized that you and your crew have done a marvelous job. One idea that has been suggested is that the entire crew be transferred to a new destroyer—one of the new Fletcher Class."

"Ridiculous! It will take two or three months to work up a new ship, even with my experienced crew. How many merchant ships will be lost while we're out learning a new ship? Is that what

Washington wants?" Another thought occurred to him: "And what about this useless 'hunter-killer' foolishness? The group hasn't 'hunted and killed' a single U-boat! Sometimes I feel like *Woodside* is the only one out there that is accomplishing anything!"

Sigsbee nodded:

"Yes, I want to talk you about the hunter-killer thing, too." He paused thoughtfully, then turned to Jamison:

"Jamison, can you estimate how long it will take to repair this ship?"

"I can only guess at this point, but I'd guess two to three weeks."

Ed spoke sternly:

"So—we can have *Woodside* back to sea in three weeks instead of three months for a new ship—that seems like a pretty clear decision to me!"

Sigsbee was thoughtful, and then turned to Jamison:

"How soon can you get her in drydock?"

"Should be by Friday, then we can find out for sure what she needs. And to answer your earlier question, Captain—yes, I think she's worth the time, effort, and cost to repair. This is a well-built vessel that has a lot of service left in her!"

Jamison left and Sigsbee and Ed went on to discuss the disappointing performance of the hunter-killer group. Ed described the brief success they had working with the British bomber and expressed his conviction that the team of ships plus aircraft could be a game-changer. He stressed it was not a case of the airplanes killing the subs while the ships protected the carrier, but one of closely coordinated teamwork. He also expressed his strong belief that the carrier should not embed itself in the convoy but, rather, range aggressively ahead—truly *hunting* and *killing* the U-boats.

It was a long and intense talk but, finally, Sigsbee took a deep breath and smiled:

"Ed, get into your blues—we're having dinner with your British friends."

Ed smiled and hurried to change clothes.

Tuesday
April 6, 1943
18:30
"Little Italy"
New York, New York

One of the sailors attending Mike's nuptials snapped a few pictures and he gave the roll of film to Mike. Now that the ship had returned to New York, Mike dropped the film off at Harbeck's Pharmacy on his way home. Due to the speed with which everything had happened, he hadn't been able to get a letter off telling his family his news. As he climbed the front steps and opened the front door, he was quite nervous about how the family would receive his news. He entered, closed the door behind him, and yelled:

"Hey, Ma! Pop! Anybody home?"

The sound of a crashing pan from the kitchen told him Ma had heard him. She came rushing in and hugged him tightly:

"Oh, my boy—you're home safe again!"

"Yeah, Ma—I'll tell you all about it at dinner. I mean—you didn't already eat, did ya?"

She smiled: "No, your father had to work late at the docks. What with the war and all, he works an awful lot. He should be here pretty soon, though."

Mike went upstairs and changed into his civvies. By the time he came back down, the front door opened and in came his Dad.

Mr. Torelli is a short, stout, heavily muscled man. His work on the docks is very physical and, by the time he finally arrived home in the evening, he was very tired. He looked up and saw his son smiling at him:

"Hi, Pop—welcome home!"

The older man smiled a slow smile: "Welcome home yerself!"

They shook hands as men do and Mr. Torelli looked carefully at his son:

"You look good, boy—they must feed you good on that ship a' yours."

Mike smiled. Dad looked carefully again:

"What is it, son? Something's bothering you—is the Navy giving you trouble?'"

Mike shook his head:

"Nah, I like the Navy. I'll—uh—well—I'll tell you all about it at dinner."

Soon, the men had washed up and were sitting at the table and Ma was bringing out the platters and bowls filled with food. Her men were big and strong and she fed them well.

Once the platters were passed and everyone's plate was full, Dad looked at Mike:

"OK, son—so what's this big news you have?"

Mike took a deep breath, wrung his hands, and spoke:

"Ma—Pop—I got married. In England."

There was a stony silence, finally broken by Ma quietly asking:

"Son, you really are married?"

Mike nodded.

"In a church and everything?"

"Yes, Ma."

"Is she a good Italian girl?"

"No, Ma—she's English. Remember I told you about the girl I saved from the bombing? It's her. We've been writing ever since and we see each other every time we're in Liverpool."

Ma was quiet. Dad asked:

"Is she at least a good Catholic girl?"

Mike was slow to answer:

"Yes, I think so. We got married in an Anglican church and they do everything the same as Catholics. It's like the English version of the Catholic Church."

Ma asked: "So she's been confirmed and everything?"

"Yes, Ma." Mike went on to hurriedly explain why he hadn't been able to write them. He described April, told about what a great girl she is, and ended by saying "And we love each other."

Ma looked at Pa. Both were quiet. Finally, Dad spoke:

"Son, this is shocking news. We always thought we would know the girl and we would attend your wedding. Now you've gone and married a foreigner who lives clear across the ocean. I don't know what to make of it…"

Ma asked quietly: "So will you be living in England?"

Mike smiled: "No, Ma—we're working on getting April moved over here and we'll live right here in New York."

The rest of the evening was strained.

*   *   *   *   *   *   *

As soon as he was able to leave the ship, LTJG George Radcliff headed for the O-club where he could find a telephone. After much difficulty, he placed a call to the Naval War College in Newport, Rhode Island, and asked to be connected with Miss Lucinda Wallings. The person who answered said they'd try to find her. There was a long delay until the person came back:

"Sir, I'm sorry—Miss Wallings is not here. I am told she is on temporary duty at something called 'ASWORG" which I am told is in New York City."

George was stunned, but his surprise was at his good fortune. He thanked the lady for her help and hung up. He immediately picked up the receiver again and dialed the number for ASWORG which he had noted in a small notebook he always carried. When the phone was answered, he asked to be connected to Miss Wallings. Three or four minutes passed until a familiar voice came on the phone:

"Hello—this is Miss Wallings."

George smiled:

"Hello, Lucinda—it's Prof…"

Silence. Then:

"What? Prof? Is that really you?"

He assured her it was and they soon made arrangements to meet for dinner. Prof was very happy.

*　*　*　*　*　*　*

Joey Donatelli made it home, too. He was happy to see his Ma, but he was sad that his girlfriend lived clear out in California and he couldn't even telephone her. They had been writing faithfully, but he really missed Veronica. He also wondered about how Mike's family would take their son's big news. At any rate, Joey decided to just use the time to relax and forget about the sonar and ships and the Navy for a while.

*　*　*　*　*　*　*

All of the men from *Woodside* planned to enjoy the expected two or three weeks in New York. It wasn't to be…

The planned effort to repair the ship turned out to be easier than first projected:

Rather than attempt to roll and drill new hull plates for the repair of the aft hull, it was decided to simply cut out the damaged section and weld in new plates. It was much simpler and took far less time.

The port shaft was carefully tested and measured and the run-out was fine. As a result, the new screw was mounted immediately.

The rudder, it turned out, wasn't bent—it was just tipped to one side. The workmen disconnected the hydraulic system inside the after steering room and loosened the through-hull bushing. They then could force the rudder and post back into the proper position and retighten the packing gland and bushing. The rudder stayed in position when they swung it by hand, so they then reconnected the hydraulics, correcting for any misalignment. The rudder was now fine.

The result of all this was *Woodside* was floated out the drydock mid-afternoon on Wednesday, April 14. She would go to sea the next day for underway trials. As a result, the expected two to three weeks the men had expected turned out to be about one week. Some of the men were disappointed, others simply shrugged it off.

The sea trails indicated minimal problems—the rudder packing gland needed some extra tightening, the new plates didn't leak, and the port shaft worked perfectly. *Woodside* was ready to go back to war.

Thursday
April 15, 1943
U-boat Base
Brest, France

It had been a busy month for U-115 and her crew. Following their ignominious arrival at the end of a rope as towed by the gallant S-103, repair specialists had swarmed over the beat-up submarine. Berger had to smile as one of the supervisors roamed over the boat muttering to himself with every step. He had good reason to mutter—the boat had a long list of serious damages. The boat wasn't the only thing damaged— Kapitanleutnant Heinz Folger had been diagnosed with a mild concussion and had been held in the base hospital overnight. His return to U-115 was not a joyous occasion.

Upon his release from the hospital, Folger had gone to the Flotilla Commander and filed a formal complaint against First Officer Helmut Berger, claiming Berger had failed to engage the enemy and was, therefore, derelict in his duties.

Berger was talking with the repair foreman when he received a summons to the Commandant's office. He couldn't imagine why he had been summoned, but he quickly changed into his formal uniform and reported as ordered. He was kept standing at attention before the Commandant's desk as the Commandant read off the formal charges against him. Berger was astounded!

Berger remained stiffly at attention with his eyes fixed upon the wall above and behind the Commandant but his astonishment must have shown:

"Mr. Berger, how do you respond to these allegations?"

Berger stated firmly: "Not guilty!"

"Are you disputing the claims of your commanding officer?"

"I did not fail to engage the enemy, sir!"

"Then why are you charged with this serious crime?"

Berger thought carefully before answering:

"Sir, I can only imagine it is because Kapitanleutnant Folger stated we should attack enemy shipping as we returned to base."

"And what is wrong with that?"

"Normally, nothing is wrong and, of course, we would remain actively on patrol as long as possible."

"But you did not attack enemy shipping on your way back here?"

Berger shook his head: "No, sir. Our boat had been extensively damaged and we were not in a material condition to attack. There was a very serious possibility that we would lose the boat entirely. We had no communications, we had serious damage to the conning tower, both periscopes were gone, the aft anti-aircraft gun was gone and its four-man crew was killed, the port screw was out of service and, later, the starboard screw was blown off the boat by an air attack. We were leaking fuel and were not certain we could even reach port. We couldn't submerge, we couldn't protect ourselves, and we couldn't call for help. Ultimately, we could not even move the boat. Sir, U-115 was not able to attack as Herr Folger wished."

The Commandant looked sharply at Folger:

"Is this true?"

Folger snapped:

"If I were not incapacitated, the boat would have attacked."

The Commandant looked upset:

"Folger, that is not my question! Has Herr Berger accurately described the damage to your vessel?"

Folger hesitated:

"I don't know, sir—I was incapacitated by my serious wounds."

The Commandant shook his head:

"I will investigate this more thoroughly and we will meet again at a later date. You are both dismissed!"

Folger and Berger did not walk together back to the boat.

It was exactly one week later that Berger was again summoned to the Commandant's office. Berger again snapped to attention before the Commandant's desk:

"Berger, I have concluded my investigation of the events we discussed last week. The serious nature of the damages to your boat had not been reported to me at that time. I now have a complete report—in fact, there was serious discussion regarding whether U-115 should be repaired or simply scrapped. Because the Fatherland needs every possible submarine, it has been decided to repair her."

Berger was relieved to hear that.

"In addition, I have also interviewed various of your officers and crew regarding the suggestion made by Herr Folger to make further attacks. I have compiled my report and my findings are thus: First, it is confirmed by the repairmen that U-115 was incapable of further aggressive attacks. Indeed, you are highly praised for having saved your boat and returned it here. Second, through interviews, I have learned that your conduct in the absence of your Captain meets the highest standards of the Kriegsmarine and the UBootwaffe. Therefore, I have ordered the following:

1. U-115 will be made fully ready for continued aggressive service against our enemies.
2. Kapitanleutnant Folger has been diagnosed with minor injuries that will not impede his abilities to serve his country.
3. Kapitanleutnant Folger has been reassigned to other duties that will allow him to impart his aggressive spirit to newly trained officers.
4. You have been advanced to the rank of Oberleutnant zur See.
5. You have been appointed the Commanding Officer of U-115 effective immediately."

Berger was astounded—Folger was gone and Berger now commanded U-115! Absolutely astounding!

"Thank you, sir," he stammered.

"You are dismissed."

At a meeting later, the Commandant shared with the crew of U-115 that they had a new Kapitan. Berger was both pleased and slightly embarrassed when the men cheered the news of Folger's departure and Berger's appointment as their leader. Morale soared.

The crew was divided into two groups and the first group departed immediately on their brief one-week leave. It wasn't long enough to go home to Germany, so most simply took accommodations in the area surrounding Brest and found female companionship to help them "rest".

Repairs to U-115 proceeded as quickly as available materials and equipment allowed. The numerous shell holes were quickly patched, as was the hole in the fuel blister. The hole in the conning tower was quickly welded over and the interior of the tower was stripped of debris and rebuilt. The hatches into the control room and up to the bridge were both replaced and the deformed metal of the decks was cut out and new plates welded in. The most difficult issue was the top of the tower where the periscopes had been attached and passed through to the control room. The surface was deformed, so new steel was welded in place and new packing glands and thru-fittings were installed. The problem, though, was that the new periscopes had to come from Germany and would take two weeks to arrive.

Meanwhile, another group of workers was rebuilding the after anti-aircraft gun platform. Fortunately, a new quadruple type

38/43 antiaircraft gun was available and it was installed on U-115.

By March 31, the boat was nearly complete—only two major issues remained: Fitting the new periscopes and directional antenna, and the crucial problem of the propulsion screws and shafts. Propulsion was a serious problem. There was no starboard screw and the port screw was severely bent. Replacing both was not an insurmountable problem, but the condition of both shafts was concerning. The local repair supervisor had measured each shaft and determined that the starboard shaft was salvageable, but that the port shaft was bent and would need replacement. To confirm his findings, he requested a visit from a specialist from the Krupp Works in Kiel, builders of U-115. He arrived and carefully evaluated the damages. He essentially agreed with the local man, but he suggested the most prudent action would be to replace both shafts. Much to everyone's relief, the man reported he could have two shafts shipped immediately and he also stated that two new screws would be included too. The shipment was placed as "urgent" and the goods should arrive in just a few days.

By April 14, all repairs had been completed and U-115 was scheduled for sea trials the next day. All went well, with the expected minor adjustments and leak stoppages. The boat returned to Brest on the 15th and was declared ready for patrol. In addition, her home port was changed to Brest, which suited Berger perfectly.

Friday
April 16, 1943
13:00
USS Woodside (DD-203)
Brooklyn Navy Yard

Commander Palmer had received orders for *Woodside* to depart the Navy Yard and return directly to her homeport of Newport, Rhode Island. The ship had passed her sea trials and was now fully stocked and fueled. Ed gave the order:

"Make all preparations to get underway. Set the Special Sea and Anchor Detail!"

A short while later, the only things holding *Woodside* to the pier were the fore and aft mooring lines and the gangway between the pier and the quarterdeck. She was tied up with her bow pointing out toward the East River, and she was alone at the pier—it should be an easy unmooring and departure.

Ed was about to order the removal of the gangway when a staff car raced out the pier and stopped at the gangway. Ed was not overly surprised to see his superior and friend Captain Stu Sigsbee alight from the car and race across to board the ship. Sigsbee came directly to the bridge:

"Hello, Ed—you can cast off the gangway now."

Palmer WAS surprised at that:

"Stu, you're coming with us?"

Sigsbee smiled:

"Sure—it's faster than the train!"

Ed smilingly shook his head, and then gave the order to remove the gangway. When that was completed, he gave orders to the engine room for "both ahead slow" and ordered the mooring lines cast off. The Coxswain applied a bit of right rudder and *Woodside* angled slowly away from the pier and headed toward the River. Once they were well underway, Ed secured the Special Sea Detail and turned the conn over to Lieutenant Williams. Ed and Sigsbee went below to Ed's cabin.

"Well, Stu, to what do I accord the honor of your presence?"

Sigsbee smiled:

"Besides giving me a ride home?" He paused: "Actually, Ed, there some things we need to talk about and the trip will give us time."

Ed listened:

"Ed, you did a great job of getting *Woodside* repaired in record time. That quick turn-around probably saved your ship from a fate worse than death."

"Huh?!"

"As you know, they have been taking some of your sisters and removing a couple of boilers and using the space to house troops—they call them 'high-speed transports'. Others have been converted to serve as mine layers..."

"Oh, God—not us!"

"No, as I said, you seem to have saved yourself. You won't be in Newport very long though—you have orders to return to the North Atlantic." Sigsbee seemed to gather his thoughts:

"There was a meeting in Washington a couple of weeks ago called the Atlantic Convoy Conference. Admiral King met with British and Canadian naval leaders to discuss strategy. They decided that each country will control its own forces in the Atlantic and—

"What?!" Ed was shocked: "So we'll each go our own way—no coordination between us? That's disastrous!"

"—if you'll let me continue! Henceforth, Britain and Canada will control the North Atlantic and the U.S. will control the Central and Southern Atlantic."

Ed couldn't believe what he'd heard:

"Unbelievable! I guess this goes along with our impotent 'hunter-killer' groups?"

Sigsbee glared at Ed:

"Commander Palmer, be quiet until I've finished!"

Ed nodded angrily.

"King has also created a paper organization called 'Tenth Fleet'. It is administrative only, but as part of it, it has been decided that we will implement an office similar to the British Convoy Tracking office. There will be a very high degree of cooperation and coordination between the British Office, a Canadian one, and ours. It should give all of us the precise information we need to eliminate the U-boat threat."

Ed kept his mouth shut.

"Because of your excellent relationships with the British, and because your ship is highly experienced and successful in finding and attacking U-boats, your immediate assignment is to attach yourself to an eastbound convoy and travel back to Liverpool. There, you will meet with Commander Roger Winn, of the British Submarine Tracking Room. Following your meeting with Winn, you will take aboard five Royal Navy officers and bring them back to New York from whence they will head for the new American tracking office to assist in getting communications set up."

"May I speak?"

"Have you calmed down?"

"Yes, sir."

"Go ahead."

"Is *Woodside* simply transporting these officers, or are we allowed to track and attack any U-boats we might encounter?"

Sigsbee smiled:

"Not only are you *allowed* to attack any U-boats—you are *ordered* to attack any U-boats. The voyage is intended to give these officers some first-hand experience in finding and sinking U-boats."

Ed smiled.

Sigsbee grinned:

"Captain, isn't it about time for evening chow?"

Ed looked at his watch, surprised at how much time had passed:

"Why, yes, Captain Sigsbee, it is about time to eat. Shall we adjourn to the wardroom?"

*   *   *   *   *   *   *

After dinner, the two men returned to the Captain's Cabin. Sigsbee looked troubled:

"What's up, Stu—you look bothered?"

"Yes. Well as you know, we've talked in the past about how long you've been aboard *Woodside*—it's now been two full tours plus a little. According to some in Washington, that's much too long."

Ed was disturbed to hear it was still a problem.

Sigsbee continued:

"It has been suggested that you should come ashore and help with this 'F-21 Submarine Tracking Room'."

Ed was incredulous:

"The WHAT? 'F-21' something—what on earth is that?"

"That's the name of the American sub tracking office. I don't know where they came up with the name—but the scuttlebutt is that since you're such an expert, you should be there helping."

Ed's distress was obvious.

"I know, old friend, we've managed to keep you afloat for a long time but—maybe—our luck has about run out."

Ed shook his head:

"So, has it been officially decided?"

"No, not yet—it's just an idea at this point. I guess I'd counsel you to forget about it for now and just focus on your next deployment. I'll deal with it as best I can."

"Yeah. Thanks, Stu."

Captain Stuart Sigsbee had just sat down at his desk with a fresh cup of coffee when he was told he had a visitor. The visitor was ushered into the office—announced as Rear Admiral Horace Cuthbert.

"Hello, Sigsbee. You can sit down. I'm here from Officer Personnel in Washington and we have a lot to discuss."

Officer Personnel? What in the world?

"Captain, you have under your command a Commander—Palmer, Edwin J..."

"Yes, sir."

"It has come to BuPers attention that he has not been cycled to shore duty in a very long time. I presume you are aware of that?"

"I am aware of Commander Palmer's time in station."

"I am sure you are also aware of the new Submarine Tracking Office that is being established?"

That's what I was afraid of...

"I am aware of the new office."

"Well, those of us in OP think it is high time Palmer came ashore. He would be a great asset to the new office."

Oh, brother—what lunacy!

"Sir, I must respectfully disagree."

"What?!" The Admiral was shocked that there would be any question of the proposed transfer. "I cannot imagine why anyone would disagree!"

OK, Stu—think carefully now…

"Sir, Commander Palmer is probably the preeminent anti-submarine expert we have afloat."

"Exactly—that is why he would be useful to the new ASW office."

"Sir, I must respectfully disagree. The purpose of the new office is to track enemy submarines and serving in that office would be an administrative position at best, and a glorified clerical one at worst. That would be an immeasurable loss to our efforts to find and destroy enemy submarines. Commander Palmer and his ship have destroyed more enemy submarines than probably any other American vessel afloat. It is vital that he remain in a position of seagoing authority. His skills are a resource we cannot afford to waste in the Washington cocktail circuit!"

Admiral Cuthbert was stunned:

"What did you say? 'Washington Cocktail circuit'? That is highly offensive!"

Oops—me and my big mouth!

Sigsbee calmed himself:

"Admiral, I mean no offense—I simply used that euphemism to indicate an administrative position that would remove from the front lines one of our most aggressive and experienced ASW experts."

Cuthbert paused:

"It seems this Palmer character is out there playing around with his old boat and managed to sink a couple of U-boats. That is not very impressive!"

Sigsbee shook his head:

"Admiral, that 'old boat' as you term it, has sunk at least six U-boats single-handedly and has assisted in sinking several others. There have also been numerous enemy boats damaged by Commander Palmer's ship. I would not describe that as 'playing around'!"

"So you disagree with the idea of rotating him ashore?"

"Yes, sir—I strongly disagree."

Cuthbert was thoughtful for a moment:

"Well, then, I will carry your concerns back to Washington."

"Thank you, sir."

"There is another matter—you."

"Me?"

"Your time in grade qualifies you for advancement to flag rank."

Uh, oh! I think I just talked myself out of a big promotion…

Sigsbee didn't respond.

"Captain, in that matter, I will also report our discussion. I do not know what might come about as a result of my report."

"Yes, sir."

Admiral Cuthbert stood, gathered his portly five-foot six-inch frame, and stomped out of the office.

What nonsense! The people in Washington seem to live on a different planet—we're trying to win a war and they're worried about who becomes an Admiral's door-opener! Amazing!

Wednesday
April 23, 1943
USS Woodside (DD-203)
Newport Naval Station

Woodside was underway and cleared Nantucket Shoals by 08:35. She then headed north—destination Halifax, where she would accompany convoy SC-128. *Woodside* steamed at an economical speed and had an uneventful voyage, arriving on April 25 just as SC-128 cleared the port and went to sea. Ed contacted the Convoy Commodore and suggested that *Woodside* steam ahead of the convoy, using her radar and sonar to assure a path clear of U-boats. His suggestion was accepted and Ed took his ship twenty miles ahead of the slow-moving convoy. SC-128 consisted of 32 merchant ships and 13 escorts. *Woodside* was not officially counted as an escort because she was "accompanying" rather than formally ordered to escort.

By Thursday, April 29, the weather began to deteriorate, which provided some respite from the U-boat danger. *Woodside's* radar and sonar remained empty until May 1 when a U-boat was located far off to port. The convoy was warned and was able to steer well clear. Aircraft were sent out and they damaged two U-boats—one of whom went missing several days later.

Shortly after this, however, the weather turned into a furious gale with high winds and high seas. On May 2, SC-128 advanced only twenty miles during the entire day and several ships straggled due to the terrible weather. Fortunately, however, because the convoy had been rerouted and because of the terrible weather,

SC-128 remained unscathed and missed the many U-boats in the area.

On May 3, *Woodside* picked up a message: Lou Garcia notified Captain Palmer:

"Captain, we just received a message from the convoy commander that we should expect to meet another convoy coming west sometime in the next day or two. They say it's convoy ONS-5, headed for Halifax. Apparently, they have had some trouble with U-boats."

"Roger. Ops Room, be on the lookout for the westbound convoy."

It didn't take long for events to deteriorate. Early on Monday, May 3, a message was picked up from ONS-5 that five of their escorts have had to leave due to low fuel. Later messages indicated that there was an increasing number of U-boats gathering around ONS-5. Ed had watched the situation carefully:

"Radar, do we have the other convoy on the scope yet?"

Miles Beckwith carefully checked his scope:

"No, sir—nothing yet."

"OK. The minute you see something, let me know!"

As the day wore on, Ed became increasingly tense:

If those subs find this convoy, we'll have our hands full. But if they find that other convoy instead, we might be able to shift over there and help. Losing five of their escorts is bad news!

On the evening of May 4, it happened:

"Bridge—Radio: I just picked up a message that a straggler from the westbound convoy was just torpedoed!"

Minutes later:

"Bridge—Radio: "Here's another one—the escorts of the westbound claim they attacked and damaged three U-boats!"

More minutes later:

"Bridge—Radio: "That other convoy is having trouble! They report they are under attack by numerous U-boats!"

"Bridge—Radar: I have the westbound convoy on my scope: Distance 20000 yards bearing 020 degrees relative!"

That made up Ed's mind:

"OK—that's it! Notify our convoy commander that *Woodside* is going the assistance of the westbound convoy. Helm—come right to 090 true! All ahead full!"

It took *Woodside* just short of 25 minutes to reach the area of the westbound convoy. It was easy to find—ships were burning like tragic beacons on the sea.

As they neared:

"Bridge—Radio: the commander of the westbound just radioed us and said "Welcome to the party! All help gratefully accepted!"

Ed had set General Quarters when they turned to go the other convoy. It was a dark, overcast night with poor visibility.

"Bridge—Radar: I have three surfaced targets bearing 005 degrees relative, distance to nearest is 3000 yards and closing!"

"Hedgehog, prepare to fire!" Ed was planning his attack as they rushed in: "Depth charges ready to roll—setting shallow!"

"Bridge—distance now 2000 yards and closing, bearing 005!"

"Helm—come right 5 degrees." He watched his bridge radar repeater; "Helm—steady as you go!"

"Bridge: target bearing 000, distance 1000 yards!"

"Guns—open fire!"

Apparently, the U-boats were concentrating on the convoy and *Woodside's* arrival was a surprise to them. The forward gun barked and barked again.

Ed could see they were getting hits on the low-lying submarine.

"Bridge: distance to next target 2000 yards, bearing 005!"

"Forward mount shift to target two! Guns 2 and 3 continue attacking target one!"

"Bridge: Target 1 is curving away to port. Target two is moving away to port in a straight line. Target two seems to be increasing speed."

While *Woodside* was trying to drive the U-boats away, other submarines were having a field day. One had attacked from the front of the convoy, then went under the entire convoy and emerged behind it where it then sank a straggler. Three other U-boats got inside the escort screen and sank four more ships. Despite these losses, the screening escorts were fighting an effective battle—so effective that U-boat leadership ordered that continuing the battle into the daylight of May 5 would require the use of submerged daylight attacks.

The first daylight attack of May 5 resulted in one ship sunk—but an escort counterattacked and sank the sub. Later, a group of stragglers was attacked but the single escort went after the sub and severely damaged it. Unfortunately, while that was going on, another sub snuck in and sank one ship. Towards evening, one of the escorts had seven U-boats in sight! A land-based B-24 tried to help but was ineffective.

Suddenly, something happened that completely reversed the tactical situation: the convoy encountered a dense fog bank which blanked the view of the attacking U-boats. The screening escorts, however, could easily find the submarines through the use of their radar and sonar. In an instant, the hunters became the hunted! The battle continued into the dark of night.

Through the night, the U-boats made 25 attacks, but all were repulsed by the escorts. Shortly before midnight, one of the escorts attacked a sub and destroyed it with depth charges. *Woodside* stayed busy, too.

Joey was on sonar and just before dawn on May 6, obtained a submerged contact. He coached the ship into position for a hedgehog attack. The attack was successful, making four explosions—and the sub was confirmed sunk. It was *Woodside's* seventh wartime destroyed U-boat.

The battle went on through the day and into the night with the escorts doing a fine job of thwarting numerous attempted U-boat attacks while damaging or sinking more subs. By morning, the German U-boat leadership learned what a disaster it had been for them and the operation was broken off. As ONS-5 continued on its westward journey, *Woodside* resumed her trip to Liverpool, arriving on Wednesday, May 12. SC-128 arrived unscathed the next day.

Friday
May 14, 1943
Submarine Tracking Room
Liverpool

The next morning, Ed went ashore and headed for London for his meeting with Commander Winn at OIC. It was an inspirational meeting.

"Commander Palmer, welcome! I have been looking forward to meeting you—please sit down."

Following a few moments of welcoming conversation, Winn got to the point:

"Commander, I understand your ship took part in the ONS-5 battle?"

"Yes, we were accompanying SC-128 when we heard the radio reports of the initial attacks on ONS-5. Because we were only sailing with—not escorting—SC-128, we were well ahead of the eastbound convoy. We were near ONS-5, so we went to assist the westbound convoy."

Winn smiled:

"My information is that you sank one U-boat and chased off two more...good show!"

"Thank you."

"Are you aware of the details of the entire battle?"

"No, sir."

Winn went on to describe, in detail, the momentous battle for the convoy. When he finished, Ed could only smile and shake his head:

"Commander Winn, that is astounding! I can't help but think back to the earliest convoys that didn't have any escorts until they neared England, and even then might only have one! Things have certainly changed—the escorts for ONS-5 did a marvelous job! Marvelous!"

Winn smiled:

"We have been building escort vessels at a rapid rate and now each convoy can have a dozen or more. Our equipment is better and our tactics are better, and the proof is what happened with ONS-5. But that is not the only success—throughout the Atlantic, we—along with you—have been making serious inroads into the U-boat fleet. I believe this month may be the breaking point for Herr Doenitz."

"I can only pray that is true!"

Winn paused:

"Now, about the gentlemen you will be carrying back to the U.S— I understand you will be sharing your expertise with them as you sail?"

Ed smiled:

"Commander—if ONS-5 is any indication, rather than *sharing with* your officers, I might well be *learning from* them!"

Winn laughed.

"At any rate, Commander, the officers will board your ship on Sunday evening. You will depart Monday morning, accompanying ONS-8."

Ed asked for clarification:

"Accompanying?"

"That's right—'accompanying'. You will be free to maneuver however you wish."

Ed smiled.

The two men enjoyed a congenial lunch and after eating, Ed received a guided tour of Winn's Submarine Tracking Office. It was impressive.

* * * * * * *

The minute liberty was announced, Mike Torelli raced off the ship and hurried to find April. She and her parents had been busy determining what was required for her to emigrate to the United States. Although it wasn't a simple process, they were making headway on the British requirements. It would, however, take Mike's assistance with regard to the American side. Finding enough time under the constraints of *Woodside's* short time in port was certainly a problem. April was able to take the rest of the day off from her job in the Liver Building and the couple went to the United States Consulate office on Paradise Street. They obtained a list of the required documents and found that April had most of them with her. That speeded the application process but some vital parts were missing. Mike learned that he was required to provide several approvals from the US Navy and no final visa could be granted until those were in place. There was also the problem that no regularly scheduled passenger ships were in public service—all were assigned to carrying troops. Even if the young couple could get the necessary paperwork together, it didn't look like April would be going anywhere any time soon.

*　*　*　*　*　*　*

Ed was back aboard late Saturday evening and was happy to receive his five visitors late Sunday afternoon. They spent the rest of the day getting acquainted and Sunday night, Ed's officers managed to make room for the added bodies. On Monday morning, May 17, *Woodside* steamed out of Liverpool ahead of ONS-8 and headed up around Ireland and out to sea. As they sailed along, Ed and his guests enjoyed a lively discussion regarding the hunting of U-boats, and especially about the possible effects of the recent success of the ONS-5 escorts.

Saturday
April 17, 1943
03:00
U-115

Helmut Berger was enjoying his new role as captain as the U-115
prepared to get underway on its first patrol under his leadership.
The boat had been repaired and even improved, and his crew
was in excellent spirits. Berger noted some changes from their
last departure, however. This time, U-115 departed in the
darkest portion of the night and was led through the mine field by
a patrol boat showing a single, dim, shaded light off her stern.
No bands played as the submarine departed; no crowd of pretty
girls waved goodbye; no high-ranking officers saluted the
departing boat. Berger felt like he was sneaking out to sea,
which, in effect, he was. The British and American air patrols
had become annoyingly aggressive to any boats caught in the
Bay of Biscay and several boats had been damaged and some
sunk. As a result, U-115 and her sisters were now required to
slip out at night. And even that was sometimes not enough due
to the patrol aircraft utilizing a high-intensity light to highlight and
attack the U-boat during even the darkest hours.

At dawn on Sunday, a British Sunderland was detected by the
onboard Metox radar detection set in time for Berger to
submerge and avoid a confrontation. Nearly an hour later, he
was able to resurface and increase speed. At 09:12, U-115 was
on the surface, maintaining a good 12 knots when, without
warning, the after anti-aircraft gun began firing furiously. As
Berger snapped his head around to see what was going on, the

146

starboard lookout screamed "aircraft!" and pointed toward the aft starboard quarter.

Berger watched as the Wellington bomber dropped out of the low clouds and made a diving approach toward U-115. It had been lurking just above the clouds until it could make this surprise attack. He watched in fascination and he felt totally helpless as two bombs fell and arced toward his boat. The projectiles struck the sea about 3 meters from the aft starboard side and—to Berger's astonishment—BOUNCED off the sea and flew over the boat to splash harmlessly in the sea off the port side!

The gunners weren't distracted, though, they continued to pour fire into the attacking airplane. The Wellington climbed away to port and turned into a steep banking turn to the left when, suddenly, the airplane fell into the sea. Berger's gunners cheered.

As U-115's course angled away from the European landmass and into the empty vastness of the Atlantic, Berger was able to maintain a good surfaced speed and they reached their patrol area a week later without further trouble.

Upon her arrival on Saturday, April 24, U-115 was attached to "Wolfpack Star" and began her patrol. There were no contacts until April 28 when U-650 reported a westbound convoy. Berger hurried to get U-115 into position, but it was well after dark when he was ready to make an attack. The convoy escorts were extremely active and Berger thought they had probably detected the U-boats. He finally managed to get into position and fired one torpedo at a medium-sized oiler, but the distance was too great and he missed. To Berger's chagrin, two of the other members of the wolfpack were caught by the escorts and were seriously damaged and had to return to port.

The war here has changed dramatically, he thought to himself, *since the days when we were free to attack at our leisure—these escorts have become dangerous!*

During the early daylight hours of Thursday, the 29th, Berger kept U-115 submerged, but in proximity to the convoy. At 09:30, he was able to penetrate the escort screen and fire two torpedoes at a 6,000-ton freighter. One torpedo missed, but the other did its job and the ship slowly sank. At the same time, however, one of the other U-boats was attacked and damaged by the escorts and it, too, had to return to port. That was three boats damaged in two days!

As Thursday wore on, the weather began to deteriorate dramatically. By nightfall, there was a tremendous gale blowing and the boats were not able to maintain contact with the convoy.

The next day was spent submerged as a way to stay out of the turbulent weather. On Saturday, May 1, a broadcast from headquarters announced the presence of an eastbound convoy approaching the area, and all boats were ordered to converge there. U-628 reported contact with the new convoy and Berger set out to rendezvous with them and the other boats. As the boats gathered, however, the convoy turned away and avoided them. Worse yet, allied aircraft arrived and attacked the submarines—two were damaged and one of those later sank.

In the evening of Monday, May 3, another report arrived regarding an approaching convoy which, due to the weather delays, turned out to be the same westbound that the wolfpacks had lost contact with a couple of days earlier. The boats formed up again and prepared to attack. There was a report of a single escort traveling well ahead of the convoy, but it was not expected to be a danger. This time, U-115 was attached to "Wolfpack Fink", which consisted of 28 boats. Two other wolfpacks contained an additional 13 boats.

This must be the most U-boats ever assembled to attack a single convoy! We'll wipe out the entire thing! Berger was ecstatic.

First blood was gained by U-125 late on May 4, who sank a straggler. Three other boats attempted to attack the main convoy but were damaged. Two had to return to port—the other would attempt to manage repairs. The escorts were fighting valiantly and the U-boats were having trouble penetrating the screen. Early on May 5, though, the vast number of submarines began to prevail and the convoy defense collapsed. U-115 closed in and fired three torpedoes at a large freighter and she quickly sank. U-707 boldly attacked from the front of the convoy, then dove under the convoy and reemerged at the rear where she sank a straggler. Other boats moved in and a furious attack ensued. Within 15 minutes, four ships were sunk and the U-boats continued to make submerged attacks. Another ship was destroyed at 04:28. In the midst of all this, a message came in from Admiral Doenitz that made Berger smile—the message encouraged the U-boat commanders to press home an attack whenever an opportunity presents itself.

As though he needs to tell us that! What does he think we're doing—watching as these ships sink themselves?

Numerous submerged attacks continued throughout the day. Berger moved U-115 into position to fire at a large freighter, but an escort rushed at him and he had to divert from his attack. By the time Berger could attempt to get back into position, the convoy was pulling away and his submerged speed wasn't sufficient to catch up. His packmates, however, were still scoring—one ship was sunk at 14:00, another at 16:43, and U-266 sank three more at 21:50. The U-boats did not get off unscathed, however—one more submarine was sunk and two others were seriously damaged. As darkness deepened, there were still at least 15 boats in contact with the convoy. At that moment, however, something happened that changed the entire battle—the convoy entered a dense fog bank!

Just when the U-boats expected to overwhelm the escorts, they suddenly could not see the enemy! The escorts, on the other hand, could easily still track the U-boats with radar. In an instant, the entire tactical picture reversed.

Through the evening, the U-boats continued to attempt attacks, but all were repulsed. As the night wore on, other subs were damaged and some were sunk. By morning, additional escorts arrived and drove off the remaining submarines. The final score: ships sunk= 13; U-boats sunk= 6; U-boats damaged= 7. The battle turned out to be the greatest single loss of U-boats so far in the war.

U-115 was one of the boats that was not damaged and was able to remain on patrol. In the days that followed, two additional convoys passed by and Berger tried mightily to make an attack. On Sunday, May 9, the closest attack he was able to manage resulted in a surfaced attack on a straggler using the forward deck gun. Strikes were made, but the ship steamed hurriedly out of range. On Tuesday, May 11, he tried to make a submerged attack on a freighter, but the range was too great and he aborted without firing.

Saturday
May 15, 1943
U-115

On Thursday, May 11, Berger received orders to move eastward into patrol quadrant AL in order to intercept three convoys steaming from Liverpool to Halifax. U-115 arrived at her new station on Friday evening, May 12. For the next three days, Berger patrolled generally in an eastward direction, hoping to intercept the oncoming convoys. Just before dark on the 15th, his patience was rewarded—he spotted a large convoy heading west. The problem was, he was too far south. Aware of the ship's radar, he had U-115 ballasted low in the water. He immediately put on speed and headed northward as fast as U-115 could go when more than half submerged. It was after dark when he finally approached the convoy. The first thing he noted was that it was protected by 12 escorts. He also detected that he might be able to sneak in and get off at least one salvo of torpedoes. He watched the nearest escort steam quickly past and noted the next destroyer was well behind the first. It was now time to fully submerge and make his approach.

"Hold her at 18 meters! Speed seven knots! Ready forward tubes!"

Berger had the periscope positioned just high enough to be out of the water and he swiveled repeatedly watching the escorts and the merchant ships ahead of him. It was a tense ten minutes, but U-115 had successfully passed within the escort screen.

"Come left ten degrees! There—steady on your course! Prepare to fire tubes one and two on my signal!"

He was aiming at a medium-sized freighter he estimated at 5000 tons. It was low in the water, so it was obviously loaded. He waited as the boat closed to an acceptable firing position.

"Slow to three knots! Maintain present heading!"

He watched as his target steamed slowly across in front of him. He judged how far to lead it and when all looked good—

"Fire one! Fire two! Hard right rudder—"

He had just ordered the turn when U-115 was rocked by a close explosion. The torpedoes hadn't completed their runs yet, so he spun the periscope and, to his horror, saw a destroyer coming fast and nearly on them.

"Take her deep! Crash dive! Crash dive!"

He continued his turn intending to leave the area. Another series of explosions shook the boat and shattered light bulbs.

"Hard left rudder!"

Berger hoped the abrupt course change might confuse the destroyer. At that moment, he heard and felt the explosion of one or both of his torpedoes.

"Kapitan—the destroyer is past us and is turning to starboard!"

"Hard starboard rudder! What is our depth?"

"Kapitan, we are passing through 90 meters!"

"Level her off at 100."

"Sir, the destroyer has passed by us and is off to our starboard side and is moving away!"

"Right! Helm, give me twenty degrees left rudder!" Berger watched the swing of the compass: "Rudder amidships—steady as you go!"

U-115 continued quietly away from the convoy. Berger was beginning to think they might actually escape the escorts. Minutes passed and no further attacks materialized and he realized they had somehow managed to elude the enemy.

Much later, Berger ordered U-115 to the surface and he radioed headquarters that they had sunk one ship. The fresh air flooding into the boats was greatly welcomed by all.

Berger was on the bridge when the radioman asked permission to join him. That was unusual and Berger wondered what was so important.

"Sir," the young sailor began hesitantly, "I have been keeping track of our sister boats and I have noticed something startling."

Berger looked at him quizzically.

"Sir, as best as I can tell, there have been nine U-boats lost in the past week—several of them from this area where we are patrolling."

Berger was shocked:

"Are you certain of this?"

"Sir, it is unofficial, of course, but I keep track of our sister boats when they report to headquarters. When time passes and a boat is not heard from, that usually means that boat has been sunk."

"I see. Thank you for your report."

Berger was distressed at the news. He knew the enemy had become much more proficient in attacking the boats, but he had no idea the situation was so bleak.

Nine in the past week added to the six that were sunk by that recent convoy—that's fifteen boats in two weeks!

 He decided that all he could do was to be careful and to make his attacks intelligently.

Tuesday
May 18, 1943
USS Woodside (DD-203)
55.25N X 21.40W

Woodside was steaming at twenty knots on a course of 285 degrees, well ahead of ONS-8. The bridge was crowded with the addition of the five extra bodies, but the men were enjoying the voyage and the lively discussions as they sailed along. Prof had encouraged the men in the Ops Center to be especially vigilant—he wanted to make sure they presented themselves well to their visitors.

The weather was surprisingly nice—a bit cold with the temperature in the mid-40s, but the sky was generally clear and the sea condition was moderate-to-light swells. *Woodside* steamed along in her normal rolling and pitching attitude and Tuesday, the 18th, passed uneventfully.

Wednesday, May 19 began as a copy of the previous day—until, at 13:23, Miles Beckwith picked up a faint contact on radar.

Berger had spent the past two days fruitlessly patrolling, hoping to contact the next convoy that headquarters had reported coming toward them. He continued in an easterly direction, hoping to meet the oncoming convoy. He remained on the surface as much as possible so he could find the convoy at the greatest range—he was confident the Metox unit would warn him of any radar searches. Being on the surface gave him greater speed if necessary, and also had the benefit of keeping the boat filled with fresh air. Berger was thoughtful as they motored along:

So far, my first patrol as Kapitan has been relatively successful— three ships sunk. We have been attacked but have not been harmed. And now this large convoy is supposed to be coming right at us—I would love to sink at least two ships, but—who knows what might happen! U-115 is a good boat with a fine crew and I don't want to let them down…

U-115 pitched and rolled as she always did on the surface. Her equipment operators were diligently on the job and the lookouts were searching carefully. The boat continued heading eastward.

The next day, Wednesday, May 19, saw Berger becoming increasingly tense. He felt that this would be the day they would find the reported convoy and he wanted to do well. So far as he could tell, there were no other U-boats anywhere in the area, so any success was up to him. He wasn't surprised when, just after 13:20, the soundman reported the sound of distant screws— probably a destroyer.

Berger wondered why the Metox hadn't detected any radar signals, but he would deal with that later.

"Get everyone below! Prepare to submerge!"

Wednesday
May 19, 1943
13:24
USS Woodside (DD-203)
55.25N X 22.40W

"What have you got, Mr. Radcliff?"

"Sir, probable surfaced U-boat bearing 003 degrees, 15000 yards."

"Thank you. Set General Quarters!"

The raucous alarm reverberated throughout the ship and the pounding of many feet signaled the hurried movement of crewmen to their battle stations. In moments, all stations had reported they were manned and ready.

"Bridge—Radar: the sub seems to be submerging—I'm losing the radar signal!"

"Bridge—Sonar: I have a submerged submarine bearing 002 degrees, distance 13000 yards!"

"Prepare for hedgehog attack followed by depth charges—set the charges for shallow."

Wednesday
May 19, 1943
13:40
U-115
55.25N X 22.40W

"Level off at 20 meters! Prepare all tubes! Up scope!"

Berger knelt as he grasped the periscope handles as the scope raised. He immediately saw the oncoming destroyer.

"Destroyer approaching! Prepare to fire tubes three and four!"

Berger was puzzled, though:

Why is there only one escort? Where is the rest of the convoy?

He quickly swung the periscope around through the entire 360-degree circle—there were no other ships.

Only one destroyer? He thought about it: *Is this some sort of a trap?*

"Come right two degrees!"

Are there any aircraft?

He searched the sky carefully and could see no airplanes.

I don't know what's going on, but if I can sink this ship, so much the better!

Minutes passed as the ship drew closer. Berger watched the enemy's movements carefully as he planned his attack.

As the ship neared, he suddenly noticed something that made him smile:

"Ah!" He exclaimed: "This ship is our old friend number 203! We meet again!"

Berger took his time and coached his boat into a perfect firing position:

"Fire three! Fire four!"

Wednesday
May 19, 1943
13:40
USS Woodside (DD-203)
55.25N X 22.40W

"Bridge—Sonar: Submerged submarine bears 000 degrees, 2000 yards."

"Roger."

Then, suddenly, Sonarman Wirtz yelped:

"Bridge—high-speed screws! It sounds like two torpedoes in the water! Bearing 000 degrees, closing fast!"

Ed was painfully aware of the wide and slow turning characteristics of his ship, but he judged he had time to jog aside of the incoming torpedoes:

"Hard right rudder! Full ahead!"

He watched the painfully slow beginning of the course change and he also watched the bubble trail of the incoming fish. He timed the command, and then yelled:

"Hard left rudder!"

He watched as the ship curved slowly to the left, but it looked as though the torpedoes would miss. He didn't want to overcorrect and put himself back in harm's way, so he barked:

"Rudder amidships—steady as you go!"

The others on the bridge held their breaths as the ship slipped out of the path of the torpedoes and both passed harmlessly along the port side.

"Bridge: U-boat bears 356 degrees, 1000 yards."

"Stand by for hedgehog attack!"

Wednesday
May 19, 1943
13:40
U-115
55.25N X 22.40W

Berger swore as the destroyer nimbly sidestepped his first salvo. He now needed to prepare for the expected depth charge attack, but he was also planning his next attack on the enemy ship.

"Full right rudder! Take her down to 30 meters! Prepare for depth charge attack!"

Once he passes over, I'll swing out to the right and get a good broadside shot at him!

He let the boat swing away from the attacking ship. He would then turn sharply and reverse his course.

Wednesday
May 19, 1943
13:42
USS Woodside (DD-203)
55.25N X 22.40W

"Bridge: sub has turned to our port, bearing 350 degrees, distance 800 yards!"

"Full left rudder! Sonar, coach us to him for a hedgehog attack!"

"Bridge, continue turning. OK, ease your turn—easy—a little more—there! Steady as you go! Sub bears 000 degrees, 300 yards!"

"Hedgehog—standby!"

"Bridge, distance 250 yards!"

"Fire hedgehog!"

The rapid-fire popping of the hedgehog projectiles being thrust ahead of the ship had everyone's attention as they waited for the hoped-for contact explosions.

Wednesday
May 19, 1943
13:43
U-115
55.25N X 22.40W

Berger waited as his boat swung out from the destroyer's path. He was visualizing his beam attack when suddenly, there was a violent explosion.

"What the...?"

Reports came immediately that the overhead in the Petty Officer's quarters was deformed and there was minor leakage. The repair crew hastened to subdue the leakage.

How did that happen? They hadn't passed over us yet, so it can't be a depth charge. Besides, that didn't sound like a depth charge explosion. What do they have now??

"Full right rudder! Prepare for depth charge attack!"

Wednesday
May 19, 1943
13:44
USS Woodside (DD-203)
55.25N X 22.40W

Ed rejoiced when he heard the single explosion of the hedgehog projectile, but he knew one might not be enough.

He timed his command, then:

"Roll depth charges!"

The big cans rolled off the stern and the Y-gun launched smaller versions out to the side.

Wednesday
May 19, 1943
13:45
U-115
55.25N X 22.40W

Berger had turned the boat away as soon as the other explosion occurred. It was a good thing.

The depth charges went off slightly above the lurking submarine and U-115 was forced violently downward. There were more reports of leaking valves and pipes, but nothing too serious. Berger knew the destroyer was now deaf for a few moments and it would circle away to clear the disturbed area. He took advantage of that and brought the boat back up to periscope depth. He extended the tube just enough so he could see his attacker. His relative position was awkward, but not impossible:

"Come left ten degrees! There—steady as you go! Fire one! Fire two!"

Wednesday
May 19, 1943
13:46
USS Woodside (DD-203)
55.25N X 22.40W

The port lookout yelled:

"Torpedo, bearing 300!"

Ed looked and saw two more torpedo tracks coming toward his port bow. The angle indicated they had been fired from slightly behind amidships.

Engines all Stop! All back emergency!"

Ed hoped the ship would stop and begin to back up in time for the two torpedoes to pass ahead. He held his breath as the missiles neared *Woodside.* Good fortune held and they passed just ahead of the bow.

Whew!

"Bridge: sub bears 260, 1500 yards!"

Engines all stop! Full ahead both! Full left rudder!"

Ed planned to make another hedgehog attack and headed the ship in that direction.

"Bridge: sub bears 395, distance 750 yards!"

A moment later:

"Sub bears 000, distance 300 yards!"

Ed paused a heartbeat, then shouted:

"Fire hedgehog!"

Wednesday
May 19, 1943
13:47
U-115
55.25N X 22.40W

Berger was disappointed that the ship had dodged his torpedoes. He was about to fire his other forward tubes when the ship suddenly started coming right at him.

"Full left rudder!"

The boat had just started to turn when there were two violent explosions behind the conning tower. U-115 rocked nearly on her beam-end and shuddered as a child shakes a rattle. Men were thrown from their footing and people sprawled throughout the boat. The damage reports began coming in:

"Engine room is flooding!"

"Main air induction flooding!"

"Air compressor room is flooding!"

Berger knew U-115 had been substantially damaged.

"Can the flooding be controlled?"

After a couple of moments, the Chief of the Boat replied:

Shaking his head, he sadly reported, "No, sir."

Wednesday
May 19, 1943
13:48
USS Woodside (DD-203)
55.25N X 22.40W

The men aboard *Woodside* all heard the two hedgehog explosions. Len Wirtz, on sonar, reported:

"Bridge, I hear sounds of flooding in the sub. It seems to be rising slowly."

"Roger—keep reporting."

"It's still coming slowly up. I think they might try to surface."

"Where will it come up?"

"A little off out starboard stern."

"Helm, turn the ship around—if that sub surfaces, I want as many guns to bear as possible!

Wednesday
May 19, 1943
13:51
U-115
55.25N X 22.40W

Berger shook his head disappointedly. But the boat was badly hurt—all lights were out, there was serious flooding aft, the engines and motors were useless. He sadly decided it was time to give up:

"Blow all ballast! Prepare to surface! Prepare to abandon ship!"

Wednesday
May 19, 1943
13:54
USS Woodside (DD-203)
55.25N X 22.40W

"It's still rising slowly…wait! They're blowing ballast! She's going to surface!"

"Guns—I want every gun possible to bear, BUT—do NOT fire unless fired upon or on my specific order! I repeat, do not fire unless fired upon or on my order!"

The men on the bridge could see the area of disturbed sea, now located about 200 yards off the starboard bow, and watched it expectantly.

Wednesday
May 19, 1943
13:55
U-115
55.25N X 22.40W

"First Officer, find me something to use as a white flag."

The man scowled at him:

"You can't surrender! We must go down fighting as loyal German officers!"

Berger shook his head:

"That would achieve nothing. Our boat is sinking. We would achieve nothing by attempting to fight a destroyer—especially an apparently undamaged one. No—I will not needlessly sacrifice the lives of these brave crewmen. They deserve a chance at a future life. Now hand me a flag!"

As it rose towards the surface, U-115 was assuming a greater and greater bow-up attitude. The flooding aft was upending the boat. Berger realized that if they didn't reach the surface soon, they might well be dragged back into the depths of the sea.

"Men, when we reach the surface, I want you all to get out of the boat as quickly as possible! She won't remain on the surface long!"

Moments later, Berger received the report:

"Sir, I think we're surfaced—at least, as best I can tell!"

"Thank you."

Berger climbed into the conning tower and opened the topside hatch. At least the conning tower was out of the water…

He climbed onto the bridge and waved the large white tablecloth as a flag. No shots rang out, so he called down:

"Get the men out of the boat quickly in any way possible!"

Suddenly the bow of the submarine lurched out of the water and soared up, much as a dolphin leaping. It settled back into a splash of white froth. In a moment, a man waving a large white flag appeared on the conning tower.

"Talker—is there anyone aboard who speaks German?"

Before the man could answer, one of the British officers, Lieutenant Ransome, responded:

"Yes, sir, I speak German."

Ed handed him the powered loudhailer:

"Order him to get his men topside. No funny business or we'll blow them out of the water!"

The German indicated he understood. Men started pouring out of the crippled submarine, some from the forward deck hatch, some from a hatch just behind the conning tower that was barely above water, and some from the conning tower itself. All soon gathered on the foredeck.

"Bosun, let's get a couple of boats over there and take them off. I want armed men in each boat. Mr. Cresswell—I want you and Mr. Adams to be prepared to go over there and search the sub. I want any classified material, code books, code machines, whatever you can find."

In less than five minutes, the two boats neared the crippled submarine and began taking the sub's crewmen aboard.

Berger knew there were 48 crewmen aboard, including himself. He remained on the conning tower and watched as his men were transferred to the boats and taken to the destroyer. While counting them, he noted that only three of his men seemed injured, and those injuries seemed minor—the men were hobbling with assistance, but they were at least mobile.

When the boats returned for the second—and last—load, Berger slipped down to the deck. He assisted the last of his crewmen into the boat and then turned, facing aft. He stood to attention and saluted his valiant craft. That craft was notably dropping lower in the water. One of the sailors called out:

"Kapitan, if you do not want to swim, you had better hurry into the boat!"

Berger took one last look at his sinking submarine, then turned and clambered into the boat.

Ed watched the scene and was poignantly touched—he could imagine if it was him stepping off *Woodside.*

All of the Germans had been gathered on *Woodside's* fo'c'sle where they were carefully searched. That task had just been completed when one of the Germans called out. Everyone turned and watched as U-115 made her last dive as she dropped stern first and slid beneath the waves.

Wednesday
May 19, 1943
14:16
USS Woodside (DD-203)
55.25N X 22.40W

Ed turned to Mr. Cresswell and the Chief:

"Well, men, obviously you won't be boarding the submarine. Chief, take the prisoners and divide them the way we did the last bunch.

"Aye, aye, sir!"

"Radio—send an urgent-immediate message to headquarters. Tell them we sank a German submarine and have the entire crew of 48 men aboard. Indicate we do not have adequate space or provisions to care for 48 extra people for a prolonged period and ask their direction."

"Helm—resume our base course."

It was over an hour later that a message was received giving directions for *Woodside.* They were told to steam at no more than 15 knots to a set of coordinates where they would rendezvous with a "Rescue Ship". The rendezvous was scheduled for 07:00 tomorrow.

"Rescue Ship? Ed asked; "What's a rescue ship?"

Lieutenant Ransome responded:

"Captain, the large convoys are now being accompanied by a converted freighter—generally about 1500 tons—that is equipped to handle crews rescued from sunken ships. They have berthing, feeding, and medical capacity."

"Well, that sounds perfect for what we need. Thanks."

Ten minutes later, Ed was surprised when Mr. Cresswell again appeared on the bridge:

"Captain, I'm sorry, but the captain of that sub wants to meet you."

"How interesting." Ed remembered the last sub captain he had met and he well remembered the arrogance of the man. "Oh, well, bring him in."

Berger was led by Cresswell, who was armed with a sidearm. Berger stepped before Ed and offered a naval salute—not the Nazi stiff arm. Ed returned it as a sign of respect. Standing before Ed was an average-sized man, probably in his late '20s, wearing a soiled naval uniform, whose blond hair needs cutting and whose blond beard was unkempt.

"Good afternoon. Do you speak English?"

Berger smiled:

"Nein. I have few words—English—from university."

Ed turned to the English officer:

"Will you translate for us?

"Of course."

"What is your name?"

Berger stood straighter:

"Helmut Berger, Oberleutnant zur See, Kapitan, U-115!"

Ed turned to the Englishman:

"Please tell this submariner that so long as his men cause no trouble, they will be treated well."

Berger smiled at the news. He smiled even larger as he began to speak:

(Translated) "Captain, you probably do not know it, but we have met before."

"Met before? When? Where?"

Berger smiled again:

"The first time was near Newfoundland where you damaged our loading hatch and we had to abort our patrol and return to base. The next time was off New York when we dueled with three of you. We put a big hole in your bow with our deck gun. The next time was when you broke into our wolfpack—you sank one of our sisters—and you got away. The last time was when you ran down behind three of our boats firing your guns. You did much damage. We were the third boat in line and we were shooting at you when one of your large-caliber shells penetrated our conning tower. Our captain was wounded."

Ed remembered the encounter well:

"Yes, and your fire wounded me, too." He stretched his neck and showed Berger the scar.

"Yes. And you blasted our rear gun completely off the boat and wiped the periscopes right off the conning tower. We pulled out and headed for port, but we were attacked by aircraft and further damaged. Finally, we were towed to Brest for repairs. This is our first patrol since then and my first in command. So you see— we have met several times before."

Ed nodded. He remembered each of the encounters but, of course, he didn't know it was U-115. Despite the fact that the man standing before him was an enemy, Ed couldn't help but almost like the man. He wasn't arrogant and he wasn't obnoxious. He was just a good officer doing his job.

Ed decided he'd tell Berger about their immediate future:

'Captain, we have orders to rendezvous with a rescue ship tomorrow morning. You and your men will be transferred to that ship, presumably to be returned to the UK for imprisonment."

"Ah—not to the US or Canada?"

"No, we do not have accommodation for you and your crew for a long voyage—the ship we are meeting does."

Berger stood up straight and saluted again:

In broken English, he said: "Thank you. Good-bye!"

Ed returned the salute and Berger was led away.

179

Thursday
May 20, 1943
06:35
USS Woodside (DD-203)
55.25N X 26.10W

Griffin Stone was watching the radar when he faintly picked up a contact far ahead of *Woodside:*

"Bridge—Radar: I have a faint contact ahead bearing 005 degrees, distance 40000 yards."

Ed was on the bridge for the expected rendezvous with the rescue ship:

"Roger—keep me posted."

Minutes later:

"Bridge—the contact bears 010 degrees, 33000 yards."

"Helm, come right ten degrees."

"Bridge—I just picked up more contacts. It looks like a convoy coming toward us—there are more and more ships showing up."

"Roger."

The ships continued to close on one another. After about thirty minutes, the lookouts reported a ship on the horizon coming toward them. Stoney also reported:

"Bridge—the ship bears 002 degrees, 14000 yards."

"Signalman, use your light to attempt to reach the oncoming ship. Inquire their identification."

The clacking of the loud shutter on the big signal light was easily heard on the bridge. In moments, a flashing light from the oncoming ship was seen.

"Captain, they state they are the rescue ship *SS Zamalek*. They request our identification."

"Go ahead."

By this time, the men on the bridge could clearly see the rescue ship nearing, and they could also see the increasing number of ships visible in the large convoy that was approaching.

"Sonar—anything out there?"

Joey was on sonar. He quickly did yet another scan:

"Bridge—Sonar: Nothing, sir, except the sound of that ship's screws. My screen is clear."

"OK. Maintain a very careful watch—we don't want some U-boat to ruin our party! You, too, Radar!"

"Aye, aye, sir."

The two ships drew carefully toward each other. Ed stopped *Woodside* and allowed *Zamalek* to approach and stop 100 yards off *Woodside's* port side. The rescue ship quickly began readying to lower a large whaleboat. The captain of *Zamalek* raised a powered hailer:

"Ahoy, *Woodside*! I hear you have some customers for us…"

Ed chuckled. He lifted his loud hailer and responded:

"Yes, indeed! We have 48 of Hitler's finest for your loving care!"

"Jolly good show! Our boat will be there in a moment."

"Thank you—we appreciate your help!"

Then Ed thought of something:

"Attention *Zamalek*—what convoy are you?"

"We are SC-130."

Ed responded:

"We were ahead of ONS-8 when we came upon this wolf."

The transfer went smoothly. As Berger stopped at the top of *Woodside's* accommodation ladder, he looked up at the bridge and saw Ed watching. Berger smiled, threw another quick salute, and went down the ladder and into the now-crowded boat. Within 15 minutes, the captives were aboard *Zamalek*, the whale boat was stowed back in her cradle, and the two ships parted. Ed gave a quick double-toot on *Woodside's* whistle as they pulled away and resumed their long voyage to New York.

Friday
May 21, 1943
USS Woodside (DD-203)
At Sea

For the rest of Thursday, *Woodside* sailed peacefully along at a steady 20 knots. Radar and sonar were carefully scanning the area as the ship moved along and, surprisingly, they didn't encounter more U-boats. In fact, SC-130 had sunk four U-boats before they rendezvoused with *Woodside* and that might have thrown the subs into disarray. That changed on Monday afternoon, however—at 14.03, Griffin Stone on radar, reported a small contact located about 20000 yards away. He guessed it was a surfaced U-boat.

"What's the bearing?" Ed asked.

"235 degrees, sir."

Ed paused—he really wanted to go after that sub, but it was 10 miles in the wrong direction. He mentioned it to the British officers visiting him on the bridge. Lieutenant Ransome commented:

"Well, old boy, I agree it would be wonderful to bag another of the blighters, but..."

"But?"

"Well, captain, our little escapade with—what was it—U-115?— has put us behind schedule and, I'm sorry to say, but important people are awaiting our arrival in New York. They've said they want to rush us to Washington as soon as possible, and I'm afraid a further detour to attack this contact might not go over well."

He paused a moment, then:

"—Not that I don't think a destroyed sub is more important than we are!"

Ed chuckled, and then made his decision:

"Helm, continue on course. Radar—keep track of the target. Sonar—listen carefully in case there other wolves around."

And so *Woodside* continued on her way.

At 07:00, Tuesday, May 25, *Woodside* cleared Ambrose Light and headed into port. She sailed beneath the Brooklyn Bridge and tied up to the new Pier J at the Brooklyn Navy Yard at 10:45.

Woodside's "passengers" left the ship with salutes and handshakes and the ship's crew eagerly set about tidying up the ship and looking forward to—hopefully—generous liberty. Captain Palmer wasn't entirely surprised to see a staff car drive out the pier and to see Captain Sigsbee alight. Sigsbee rushed across the gangway and hurried to the bridge:

"Hello, Ed—don't let any of your crew leave the ship yet and I'd like an officer's meeting in your wardroom as soon as possible."

Ed chuckled:

"Well, hello to you, too! And I'll gather the officers right away—let's go below and meet them as they come in." Ed paused: "I get the impression something big has happened?"

Sigsbee responded simply:

"I'll explain when we're all together."

 A few minutes later, all were present—with coffee mugs in hand—and surprised by the immediate summons. Sigsbee regarded the group briefly, then began:

"It's good to see you men again, especially upon your return from yet another successful foray into harm's way."

They smiled.

"I hadn't planned anything other than to stop by on my way back to Newport to welcome you home—but some rather astounding things have happened."

The others now listened carefully—especially Commander Ed Palmer.

"We have recently received some fascinating and encouraging news from our British friends. As you know, from January up into March our shipping losses have been highly concerning. In fact, 108 ships were lost in just the first twenty days of March—terrible! But the good news is—the British and Canadians have worked hard to get their act together and our combined escort efforts have improved very significantly. The proof of that is that during the final ten days of March, only 15 ships were lost. In

April, only 56 ships were lost. So far this month—6 ships have been lost—just six!"

The men were now hanging on his every word.

"I imagine Commander Palmer has shared with you the establishment of carefully delineated areas of participation for the Brits, Canadians, and us. The sharing of intelligence, ease of communications, and highly coordinated activities are beginning to make a tremendous difference against the Atlantic U-boats."

He paused and looked levelly at them.

"I now have some very interesting statistics for you: So far in 1943, worldwide, in January, seven U-boats were sunk. In February, eighteen U-boats died. In March, fifteen were destroyed, and in April—seventeen."

He paused to build the suspense:

"In May—through yesterday, {pause} thirty-six have been sunk— and the month is not over. Thirty-six U-boats destroyed so far this month!"

The men were astounded. After absorbing the startling news, they spontaneously applauded. Sigsbee smiled.

"So, what we have is that fewer and fewer ships are being lost and more and more U-boats are being destroyed. We have reached a turning point in the Battle of the Atlantic!"

He let the men celebrate for a moment, then held his hands up to quiet them:

"And now for the real cherry on top—we received, early today—confirmed intelligence stating that Admiral Doenitz has just ordered a recall of all his boats in the Atlantic—for the stated purpose—Sigsbee looked at a paper he was holding and read: 'to avoid unnecessary losses in a period when our weapons are shown to be at a disadvantage' and that 'the battle in the North Atlantic—the decisive area—will be resumed'."

The men were stunned speechless.

Ed commented:

"So this means we've broken the fangs of the wolves?"

Sigsbee smiled:

"Well, they seem to require some serious dental attention!"

The men laughed. As the realization of the success of their long and painful efforts was being realized, they jumped to their feet clapping and pounding each other on the back.

As the men finally quieted down, Bill Bevins asked Sigsbee:

"Sir, does this mean the subs are really beat?"

Sigsbee looked serious:

"Well, Lieutenant, it means we have gained the upper hand. Our new tools are paying off—long-range aircraft, large numbers of well-armed escorts, better communications and intelligence, and better weapons and tactics. But I have no doubt Doenitz will make every effort to regain the upper hand—we just have to make sure he fails."

Sigsbee turned to Ed:

"Commander Palmer, I would suggest you allow these officers to collect their respective crewmen and make them aware of this success. Then you may grant liberty—local liberty only, however. There is a whole lot more we'll be involved in during the next several days and we'll need to keep your crew nearby."

After the officers filed out, Stu turned to Ed:

"Ed—great job on the sub you sank! That's what, now? Seven? Eight?"

Ed smiled:

"Eight confirmed and at least two probable. Several damaged."

"*Woodside* has been busy! Good job, Ed!"

Sigsbee paused:

"Ed, I thought I was going back to Newport, but just before I left to come here, I was tagged with some additional meetings. I have to go ashore for the next couple of days. I'll stay in touch—we have lots more to talk about."

Tuesday
May 25, 1943
USS Woodside (DD-203)
Brooklyn Navy Yard

As soon as the meetings of the various shipboard divisions ended, liberty was called. Joey and Mike teamed up and headed for home and, as they walked along, they talked about the big news:

"Joey, does this thing about the U-boats mean the war is over?"

Joey smiled:

"No—I wish it did, but—no—there's still a lot of war. I think it just means we've finally got ahead of the subs—they can't just do whatever they want anymore."

"Oh. Well, that's good, anyway—isn't it?"

"Sure. I wonder, though, what we'll be doing from now on. My whole job is to find subs underwater so we can sink them. If we aren't chasing subs anymore, what will I do?"

Mike grinned:

"Hey, Joey, come with me and shoot the guns!"

Joey chuckled:

"Thanks, pal, for the offer, but I guess they'll use my training somehow. Thanks, though!"

They reached the point where they split off for their own homes:

"Hey, Mike, let's keep in touch—OK? Maybe we can go to Maloney's or something…"

"Sure, Joey. Bye!"

Mike arrived home and surprised his mother just as she was going out to the meat market.

"Hi, Ma!"

Mrs. Torelli jumped:

"Michael, you scared the bejesus out of me! Welcome home! How long can you stay?"

"I don't know, Ma—probably not very long. Can I go with you to the butcher? I can help carry it all home."

Ma Torelli shook her head:

"I won't need much help, son—the rationing is so tight and there's hardly anything to buy. Maybe I can get a pound of hamburger or something."

As Mike and his mother strolled arm-in-arm along the street, Joey reached home. As usual, he opened the front door and found Ma in the kitchen:

"Hi, Ma—I'm home!"

Mrs. Donatelli looked up in surprise and, seeing Joey, put down the big boiler pot she was using to make minestrone soup and rushed to hug him. As they sat together later sharing a quiet late lunch, Joey told his mom about the U-boat news. She listened with pride:

"Son, you had something to do with that, didn't you?"

Joey smiled: "Well—yeah, Ma—I did. I use my machine to find the submarines underwater so we can attack them."

Ma was thoughtful:

"But, Joey, I keep hearing on the radio about how the submarines sink our ships—do they ever try to sink you?"

"Well—yeah, Ma—they do. We've been in gunfights with them when they're on the surface and they've hurt our ship. One time, one of them blew a big hole in our bow—uh, I mean—in the front of our ship. The underwater ones have shot torpedoes at us, but only one actually hit us and it almost missed, so we were OK. But—yeah, Ma—it's a war out there!"

Ma looked like she might cry:

"Oh, my son!" She exclaimed.

*   *   *   *   *   *   *

That night, after Mike's Pop got home and dinner was finished, the Torelli's were sitting comfortably in the front room when Pop asked:

"Well, Mr. Married Man, what's up with your missus? She still over there?"

"Yeah, Pop. We've about finished all the paperwork—a whole lot of paperwork! The biggest problem though, is there isn't any way for her to get here."

"Why? Can't afford the ticket? You know we don't got no extra money, if that's what you're thinking!"

Mike looked down:

"No, Pop, that ain't it—it's just there's no ships she can ride to bring her here. All the ships are for cargo or troops and there's nothin' for passengers."

"So—can't you get her on that ship yer on?"

Mike was stunned:

"No, Pop! We're a Navy ship—we fight the Germans! We don't carry no people!"

Pop paused, then continued grumpily: "Well, I still think you done stupid to marry her! Why don't she marry some English guy and leave you alone!"

Mike was saddened by his father's attitude and just sat without saying more.

*   *   *   *   *   *   *

George Radcliff—"Prof"—hurried off the ship and headed for the first telephone he could find. He called the number for ASWORG and asked for Lucinda Wallings. There was a long delay until—finally—he heard her sweet voice:

"Hello?"

"Hello, Lucinda—it's George."

"Oh, George", she exclaimed happily, "where are you?"

"We just returned to the Navy Yard—can we get together?"

She laughed: "Can we get together? You'd better believe it! Can you come here?"

George smiled:

"I'm on my way!"

Leaving the Yard and hailing a cab took longer than he expected—the city was jammed and cabs were popular and in short supply. He finally made it to ASWORG, though, and went in. The Receptionist smiled:

"You must be 'George'?"

He smiled:

"Yes, Ma'am. Where might I find Miss Wallings?"

The girl grinned:

"I've already called her—she should be here in a minute."

Sure enough, moments later, the girl George thought was the most wonderful girl in the world came through the door.

"Hi, Lucinda." His smile nearly broke his face.

"Hi? All I get is 'Hi'?"

She rushed to him and buried herself in his embrace. Her muffled voice said:

"That's better!" She looked up and kissed him resoundingly.

The Receptionist smiled and looked away.

Finally, Lucinda broke away:

"Come in—Professor Stalling will love to see you, and I think the boss is here, too."

"The Boss"—MIT Professor Philip Morse—was, indeed, in his office. Lucinda knocked and was bid to enter:

"Good afternoon, Professor—look who's here!"

George stepped in and smiled:

"Hello, Professor Morse—long time, no see!"

Morse smiled:

"Well, hello, George! Indeed, it has been a while. Back from fighting the dread foe are you?"

George laughed:

"Yes, we just got back."

"I hear you were again successful—you folks sank the U-115 and captured her entire crew?"

Radcliff was surprised the Professor knew those details but—upon a moment's thought—he wasn't really so surprised after all.

"Yes—it was a bit exciting, but the techniques you and I have discussed really helped us find and stay with that sub. We damaged them severely and forced them to the surface. They abandoned ship and we picked all of them up."

"So, from the practical point of view, you think our work here is helpful?"

"Sir, I couldn't agree more! The things we've discussed have made a total difference at sea! Sir, I presume you've learned of Doenitz' order?"

Morse chuckled:

"Actually, there was a bit of a celebration over that last night!"

Morse was thoughtful for a moment:

"George, are you happy in your role aboard ship?"

Radcliff was startled by the question:

"Why—yes—of course! Pulling together a team to effectively and efficiently find and destroy enemy submarines is very fulfilling—very fulfilling, indeed!"

Morse smiled:

"Good lad!"

They left Morse and went in search of Stalling. It wasn't a difficult search—they found him in his office, standing before a blackboard that was covered with equations and diagrams.

"Hello, Professor."

Stalling started at the sudden interruption and turned:

"Radcliff! How nice to see you! Have you been away on vacation or something?"

George laughed:

"No, Professor, my ship has just returned to port. We sank another U-boat on the way back."

A look of confusion crossed the Professor's face as he regarded what George had said.

"You—ship?—oh, my—I've forgotten—you are on a ship sinking submarines?" Then he seemed to remember: "Oh! Yes! Of course! Your uniform and all! Sorry—I was deep in thought here. So you were successful against the enemy? Wonderful!"

George and Lucinda chuckled. They went on to visit with the Professor for few more minutes and then left him. As they went out the door, they could hear the scratching of the chalk on the blackboard.

Lucinda was granted the rest of the day off and the two lovers enjoyed their reunion greatly.

*　*　*　*　*　*　*

Ed Palmer decided he'd had enough of his cabin for a while, so he cleaned up and headed for New York City, planning to enjoy a good meal and some time away from the ship. He was strolling along Fifth Avenue near 33rd Street when he noted a restaurant sign hanging over the sidewalk advertising "Armando's Trattoria".

Hmm—that sounds interesting.

He stopped before the place and read the sign over the door:

"Authentic Sicilian Cuisine"

Hmm—"Authentic Sicilian" eh? Well, maybe…

He quickly scanned the menu posted in the window and decided he'd try it.

"Welcome! Would a table by the wall suit you?"

The cute girl with long black hair greeted him with a big smile.

She took him to a table along the side of the long, narrow restaurant and handed him a menu. He read it more carefully this time and realized he didn't know what he was looking at. He'd expected the usual Italian offerings, but that wasn't what he was seeing. Apparently, his confusion showed:

The girl returned: "May I answer any questions?"

Ed smiled:

"Well—I don't know where to even start…"

She grinned patiently:

"Maybe I can help you…"

She leaned over and worked her way through the menu, describing the major dishes, starting with *caponata* (an appetizer), then *maccu* (a soup), *Pasta alla Norma* (a Catanian pasta dish), and then recommending a meat-based main dish. Finally, she stood back and happily suggested for dessert, a nice *Pinolatta de Messina* (a soft, chocolate-covered pastry).

Ed was dazzled—he hadn't expected a culinary repast like this—but it sounded delicious and he simply nodded his agreement.

As Ed waited for the feast to arrive, he looked around the restaurant. He was there in the early afternoon and well after the usual lunchtime and the place was sparsely populated. He glanced at a family across the room and smiled at their energetic conversation; he noted a young couple, probably on a late lunch break, and scattered other single diners.

The dishes started arriving and he applied himself to enjoying the wonderful meal appearing before him. He had just finished his pasta when he heard a commotion and looked up to see three women coming noisily through the door. They weren't being rude, they were just greatly enjoying each other's company. Ed smiled to himself and launched into his main dish.

A few minutes later, he paused to catch his breath and let the food digest a bit. He glanced over at the three ladies and caught one of them looking at him. As he looked at her, she blushed and looked away. He shrugged to himself and went back to eating.

Suddenly, someone was standing before him—he looked up and it was the lady he'd seen looking at him.

She appeared embarrassed:

"Hello, sir. I'm sorry to interrupt you, but—

Ed waited:

"—well, this is our first time here and I noticed you must obviously know about these foods and I was wondering—well—perhaps you might help us. BUT I don't want to disturb your meal…"

Not disturb my meal? You're kidding! Ed looked more carefully and noted she was quite pretty and she seemed to be nice—and flustered. *Oh, well—my trying to help them won't take very long at all!*

"Well, Miss, contrary to appearances, I am the least-experienced diner of Sicilian food in this restaurant!" He laughed: "The reason I have this veritable feast of wonderful food is because that sweet young waitress virtually ordered for me!"

The woman looked especially embarrassed:

"Oh! I'm sorry! I was thinking you could tell us what you're having and how it tastes and then we could maybe get the same thing. Oh, my!"

"I wish I could help you, but I don't even remember the names of what I'm eating. I will say, however, that this is one of the most flavorful and delightful meals I've ever had!"

The waitress came up to them

"Hello. Is there a problem?"

Ed smiled: "Only that these nice ladies"—he indicated the three of them—"are as confused about the menu as I was. Could you assist them the way you did me?"

She smiled: "Of course!"

She walked back to the women's table and launched into her description of the foods. Ed then knew the ladies were in good hands and he returned to his meal.

It was not a quick meal—Ed took nearly an hour before he was finishing the absolutely wonderful pastry for dessert. He sat for a while to allow the food to digest.

Boy, I'll definitely need a long walk after all of that!

The bill had been placed on the table. He noted the total—

Well, now! This certainly is nothing like eating at the O-club—in many ways!

It wasn't exorbitant, though, and he left his money and stood to leave. As he passed the three women's table he was surprised when he was hailed:

"Commander—I hope you'll forgive our interruption."

The speaker was another very attractive woman. Ed judged that all three were probably mid-to-late thirties and seemed to be office workers of some sort. He stopped and smiled:

"That was no problem—I just wish I'd been able to be more helpful."

She looked briefly at her companions:

"Commander, would join us for coffee? It's our way of apologizing."

Being invited to share coffee with three beautiful women is hard to turn down!

"Well, that's most kind of you—I'm happy to accept."

He sat down in the fourth chair and smiled:

"My name is Ed…"

The first lady he met spoke:

Laughingly: "My name is Jane—Jane Wilson." She must have noted Ed's expression: "I know—I grew up being called 'plain Jane'."

Ed smiled:

"I don't mean to be out of line or anything—but you've certainly outgrown that accusation!"

She blushed: "Thank you."

The lady to her left spoke:

"Rachel."

And the third:

"Amelia."

Ed nodded to each, then commented:

"Ladies, I noted when you arrived that you are having a great time together—I think that's wonderful!"

Amelia spoke:

"Do you enjoy close friends, too?"

Ed shook his head:

"Actually—no. I command a destroyer and I can't become close friends with any of my men, even though I like them a lot. And I've been away a great deal and haven't been able to form any close friendships ashore."

Jane looked downcast: "How sad!"

Ed just nodded.

"Do you ladies work nearby?"

Rachel responded: "Jane and I work in the Waterman Building a couple of blocks away."

"And you, Amelia?"

Amelia smiled a small smile but didn't answer. It created an awkward moment and Jane quickly jumped in:

"Amelia is visiting us from out of town."

"Ah."

During wartime there are some questions you don't ask—this seems to be one of them."

"I hope you have a nice visit."

As they relaxed with each other, the conversation began to flow—on safe topics—and they enjoyed a pleasant half-hour together.

They parted and Ed headed back to the ship. It had been a surprisingly nice day.

When he got back to *Woodside,* the OOD handed him a message:

"Sir, this came for you earlier this afternoon."

Ed took the message to his cabin, took off his coat, loosened his tie, sat down, and opened the message. It was from Stu Sigsbee:

Ed, please keep Friday open. I'll meet you in your cabin at 0930.

Stu

Friday
May 28, 1943
USS Woodside (DD-203)
Brooklyn Navy Yard

The crewmen of *Woodside* enjoyed the three days of liberty following their arrival. It was not extended, nor was it leave—but they still enjoyed the pleasures of New York and their friends there—especially their lady friends.

Ed pondered what Stu Sigsbee might want to talk about. He rather dreaded the meeting because he feared for *Woodside's* future and he guessed Stu would be discussing that.

Ed was in his cabin Friday morning, having finished breakfast and the dishes had been cleared away. The steward had just brought a fresh pot of coffee and a tray of sweet rolls. A couple of minutes before 09:30, there was a knock on his door. He opened it, expecting to see Captain Sigsbee—he certainly did NOT expect to see Mr. Jamison, the yard foreman.

"Jamison! What a surprise!"

"Aye, Captain, me, too. I'm told to come to a meeting here at 9:30, so I'm here…"

"Well, come on in. There's fresh coffee and have a sweet roll if you like."

Jamison had just collapsed his bulk into the chair next to Ed when the door opened and Sigsbee entered:

"'Morning, Ed! Hello, Jamison! Is that fresh coffee I smell?"

Soon, the three men were fortified with coffee and rolls and Sigsbee got serious:

"Men, we have a great deal to discuss and to plan for. First on the agenda is *Woodside.*"

Oh, no! That's what I was afraid of!

"As we all know, *Woodside* has fought a good war—better than most ships. She's responsible for sinking at least eight U-boats and possibly more." He looked at Ed: "Ed, you've trained your crew well and this ship functions exceptionally effectively."

Ed smiled warily:

"…But?"

Sigsbee continued:

"Well, not "but" exactly—but there is more. As you know, our shipbuilding program is well underway and great numbers of new, more modern, destroyers are coming off the ways at several shipyards across the country. We—meaning we three—also know that *Woodside* is now twenty-three years old. She has been upgraded somewhat, but many of her systems are obsolete. Also, she has been knocked about a bit by the enemy. Jamison and his people have done a marvelous job of patching her up, but her age is becoming a problem."

Sigsbee paused and looked seriously at Ed:

"Ed, *Woodside* is to be retired from combat service."

Ed was deeply saddened by the news:

"So, this fine ship is now considered a relic and she'll be cut up or turned into a garbage barge or something—how sad!"

Sigsbee shook his head:

"No, Ed, she WON'T be cut up or turned into a garbage barge— she is being decommissioned as DD-203, but she'll be recommissioned as AGT-1."

"Huh? What on earth is that?"

"AGT—"Auxiliary" "General" "Teaching". She's headed for Annapolis to be used as a teaching ship. She'll be manned by trainees from the many specialty schools and led by students from the Naval Academy. She'll be training the next generations of naval leaders—and that's an honorable job!"

Ed was relieved—but he still felt the loss as though he'd lost a dear friend:

"Well, that's a relief—it's certainly better than becoming beer cans or a garbage barge. It's still sad, though."

Sigsbee looked with commiseration:

"Well, old friend, maybe this next news will take some the sting out of it—on June 9, 1943, you will find yourself in Bath, Maine at the Bath Iron Works for the commissioning of DD-632, a new Fletcher-class destroyer. She will be commissioned as—USS WOODSIDE."

Ed lost his breath:

"What?! 'Woodside'? How—?"

Sigsbee smiled:

"Ed, as of next Tuesday, Woodside—DD-203 will no longer exist. Woodside—DD-632 will come to life on June 9."

Ed was deeply touched:

"That's—that's—I—oh!"

"I know Ed, it's great news and the namesake of your fine ship will continue in essential naval service."

Sigsbee waited a moment for Ed to digest the news, then:

"Jamison, there will be a decommissioning/recommissioning ceremony at 08:30, Tuesday, June 1, right here at Pier J. The minute that ceremony ends, your crew will have to paint out, or otherwise remove, all markings of "DD-203" or "Woodside" and replace them with "AGT-1". AGT-1 does not get a name—just the type identifier."

"OK, no problem. We'll have it done in a couple of hours."

"Good man! Sometime late next week, a skeleton crew will arrive to steam AGT-1 to Annapolis."

Jamison nodded.

Sigsbee went on:

"Here's some more good news, Ed—your crew—most of them— will be transferred intact to DD-632. They will work her up and then take her to war. They are a great crew and their experience will hasten the process of getting the new ship ready,"

That made Ed very happy.

"Fellows—there is still much more: Ed, your crew will be mustered on Pier J at 08:00 on Tuesday in ranks. Uniform of the day is Dress Whites. The decommissioning ceremony will be conducted by Rear Admiral Edward J. Marquart, Commandant of the Navy Yard beginning at 08:30. Following the ceremony, Ed—your crew will remain in ranks and will be told at that time that there will be a new *Woodside* and that they—most of them—will be her crew. They will also be ordered to remove any and all personal items no later than 1200 hours that day."

Ed nodded: "OK."

"Following that announcement, Admiral Marquart will announce a number of promotions for the men of *Woodside.* Those of men of the rank of Chief and below will be handed their notice, but the Admiral will publically announce the promotions for the Officers. Following those awards, the ceremony will close and you and crew will hustle to be ready to board transport to Bath, Maine as soon after 1200 hours as possible." Sigsbee looked at Ed: "Got it?"

Ed smiled: "Got it!"

There were some things Sigsbee didn't touch on—but those were to be a surprise.

Admiral Marquart arrived with three of his staff officers and Ed and Stu Sigsbee were on the pier, awaiting the Admiral's arrival. *Woodside's* crew was gathered, but not formally lined up. Sigsbee took Ed and approached Marquart:

"Good Morning, Admiral—may I introduce Commander Edwin Palmer, Captain of USS Woodside (DD-203)"

The Admiral offered his hand and Ed noted the firm handshake. The Admiral then introduced his assistants. He turned to Captain Sigsbee:

"Sigsbee, is everything set up? Are we ready?"

"Yes, Admiral. We will call the crew to attention at 08:30. I will introduce you and you can then explain about the decommissioning of *Woodside.* At that point, you may read the official decommissioning order and order the commissioning pennant struck from *Woodside.* Following that, you can read the official commissioning order for AGT-1 and order her pennant run up the mainmast. Is that satisfactory?"

"Yes, Sigsbee—good work. This should go like clockwork. We'll announce about the crew transfer after the new commissioning?"

"That's correct, sir."

"Good. What time is it?"

One of his Aides piped up: "Admiral, I have 08:25."

The Admiral looked at Ed:

"Commander, bring your crew to attention."

When the men saw Ed approaching, they shuffled into the proper line-up. Ed moved to stand before them:

"Woodside—Atten-hut!"

The men popped to attention and Ed was proud of their fine appearance. He took his place, standing at attention before them. The proceedings moved ahead from there.

Everything went as Ed expected until the order to take down *Woodside's* commissioning pennant. Ed watched as a seaman slowly brought the battered, frayed, and stained pennant down off the mast. The man was very respectful of the pennant and he gathered it carefully into his arms as it descended. A moment later, he disappeared. Ed was surprised at how emotional it made him feel to watch that pennant being brought down. Ed expected the ceremony to continue, but there seemed to be some delay.

Ed was standing at attention ahead of his crew when he was surprised by someone breaking ranks from behind him and marching around in front of him. It was Bill Bevins, and he had something in his hands.

Bevins marched to stand directly in front of Ed. He approached, snapped to attention, and saluted. Ed, puzzled, returned the salute.

Bevins spoke:

"Captain Palmer, as the Executive Officer of *USS Woodside (DD-203),* is my honor to represent the crew. Sir, the crew and I want you to have this commissioning pennant from *Woodside* as a memento. We have been proud to have served under your excellent leadership and we want you to have this as a token of our lasting esteem." He reached out and handed the neatly folded pennant to Ed. Ed was so choked up he couldn't speak. Bevins noted that his Captain's eyes were wet. Ed finally managed to take a deep breath and compose himself.

"Thank you, Lieutenant Bevins—I am overwhelmed with emotion!"

Ed turned to face his crew:

"Men, it has been my greatest honor to lead you in combat. You are everything the Navy strives for in a ship's crew and I am overwhelmingly proud of every one of you! Thank you for this very meaningful token of your esteem—thank you!"

Spontaneously, everyone—including the Admiral—broke out in applause.

The commissioning of AGT-1 was much more straightforward and far less emotional. Once that was completed, Admiral Marquart addressed the assembled crew:

"Men, your Captain has bestowed upon you the greatest of praise—and you have earned it. Your performance has been exemplary. As a result, I have a rather exciting announcement to make: In Bath, Maine, at the Bath Iron Works shipbuilders, there is a new Fletcher-class destroyer—DD-632—which has recently been launched and is nearly finished fitting out. On June 9—next Wednesday—DD-632 will be officially commissioned—as USS Woodside (DD-632). The name of your gallant ship will live on!"

Against every regulation in the Navy, the men broke out in cheers. The Admiral smiled understandingly. He let them go for a minute, then held up his hands to get them back in order. He then continued:

"Men, I am thrilled by your excitement. Here's something else—on June 9—YOU—or, most of you, will report aboard as the first crew of DD-632."

That resulted in total bedlam. Joey cheered. Mike cheered. Everybody cheered. Prof wondered what "most of you" meant.

The Admiral finally quieted them and gave further instruction:

"Men, at the completion of today's ceremonies, you will return aboard this ship and quickly pack and remove all of your personal belongings. As close as possible to 1200 hours, you will report back here for transportation to Maine.

The men were immediately struck by how much stuff they had to corral in such a short time.

The Admiral again spoke:

"Men, we have more good news—many of you have just have received a promotion in grade. Those of you in the enlisted ratings will now be given your formal notice of advancement."

The Admiral's assistants passed down the ranks calling out names. Among many were: Donatelli—now Soundman Second Class, and Torelli—now Gunner's Mate Second Class. Phil Summers was promoted to Radioman First Class and Griffin Stone to Radarman First Class. Once all of the notices were distributed, the men came back to order and Admiral Marquart prepared to announce the Officer advancements:

"Gentlemen, when I call your name, please present yourself front and center."

He looked at his list and started reading:

"And now the officers:

"Shulman, Robert B to Lieutenant Junior Grade with duty station USS Woodside (DD-632)"

"Cresswell, Jonathan L to Lieutenant, Junior Grade with duty station USS Woodside (DD-632)."

"Radcliff, George R, to Lieutenant, with duty station at Anti-Submarine Warfare Operations Research Group, New York, New York."

"Bevins, William J. to Lieutenant Commander, with duty station as Commanding Officer, USS Woodside (DD-632)."

The Admiral paused.

George "Prof" Radcliff was shocked:

To ASWORG? What the...? Who did this? I mean—of course I'll be happy to be with Lucinda, but...

Ed Palmer was shocked to hear that Bevins had been given the new Woodside. He had already been imagining how he would get her ready and to suddenly not be aboard was incomprehensible. He felt like his heart had been wrenched out!

The Admiral resumed:

"Palmer, Edwin L. to Captain, with duty station 10th fleet, Washington, D.C"

Oh, no! This is terrible! Now I'll be the door opener for some Admiral. I wonder if I can protest... Making Captain is fine, but pushing paper? Grrr!

Admiral Marquart paused again, then resumed with a smile:

"Sigsbee, Stuart O. to Rear Admiral Lower Half with duty station 10th Fleet, Washington, D.C."

Stu Sigsbee about fell over—this was totally unexpected.

Following the ceremony, Marquart spoke with Sigsbee:

"Sigsbee, your promotion would normally be done with much more pomp and ceremony but, due to wartime needs, things sometimes happen a bit differently. Nonetheless, I am happy to have the honor of announcing your promotion. Congratulations!

"Thank you, Sir—I'm stunned!"

After all the presentations and handshakes, the ceremonies finally came to an end. It was a pleasant morning for a lot of people and a shocking one for others.

Tuesday
June 1, 1943
10:20
AGT-1
Brooklyn Navy Yard

As soon as the meeting ended, the men crowded around Captain Palmer:

"Congratulations, sir!" Carl Bascom enthused: "Best wishes in your new post!"

"Congratulations, Captain—well deserved!" From Flynn Boyd.

Then Bill Bevins faced Ed with a serious look:

"Sir, I had no idea—but thank you. I'm sure you approved this and I appreciate it very much! I'll make you proud of the new Woodside!"

Ed swallowed:

"Bill, I have no doubt you will. Go before God, my friend!"

His—now-former—officers were effuse in their well-wishes and Ed treasured their support. He finally pulled himself away and met up with Sigsbee in Ed's—former—cabin. As Ed began quickly opening drawers and packing his belongings, Sigsbee tried to console him on what should have been a great promotion:

"Ed, I knew about your promotion and I was excited to surprise you, but I certainly didn't expect mine. After reading my orders, though, I can see what's happened: you'll be the assistant to an Admiral—ME. I assure you, I don't want you opening doors or serving canapés for me! But together, we can make a real difference in Washington!"

Ed paused in his packing:

"Admiral Sigsbee, I will serve you faithfully and obey your orders to the letter. Thank you, sir."

Sigsbee was hurt:

"Ed, that's enough of that crybaby nonsense! If you really can't stand to work with me, I'm sure we can get you orders elsewhere! Now knock it off!"

The hurt and anger in Sigsbee's voice got through to Ed:

He stopped, looked directly at Stu, and said:

"Yeah, you're right, Stu—I sincerely apologize. This has all been a shock and I'm feeling sorry for myself, but that's no excuse. You have been a tremendous friend and help to me and I am truly sorry for what I just said. I hope you can forgive me. And—congratulations on your promotion! It's long overdue and well-deserved!"

Sigsbee took a deep breath:

"Ed, we have both complained loudly about the un-informed chair-warmers in Washington. Well, we are now able to—as they say—'put up or shut up'. Together, we can make a real contribution in 'fairy-tale city' by using our practical knowledge and experience to help fight the war. That is—if you will..."

Ed hung his head, and then looked directly at his friend and mentor:

"Of course, Stu—and I mean it when I say I'm sorry. And—yes— I think we can team up to wake up some of the cocktail circuit to reality! I understand and—yes—I'm very ready to work with you—or for you—in any way I can help."

Sigsbee laughed—which surprised Ed, who looked questioningly:

"I'm sorry, Ed, but your phrase 'cocktail circuit' hits a nerve. After you left for this latest patrol to England, one of the 'chair-warmers' appeared at my office and proceeded to tell me how much the anti-sub office needed you. I protested vigorously and, in the process, used that very term to describe some of our Washington compatriots. Admiral Horace Cuthbert took great offense at my comment—I figured my chance of promotion just dropped below zero. I guess wonders never cease!"

Ed laughed. Sigsbee laughed. The men looked at each other and both knew that all was now well between them. They shook hands firmly.

Sigsbee commented:

"You'd better get back to packing—our chariot awaits us at noon!"

"So we're going to the 'Emerald City'?"

Ed was surprised by the answer:

"What? No, sir—we're traveling with your crew to take part in the commissioning of the new USS Woodside in Maine! They can't commission that ship without you! Hustle-up!"

There was a frenzy of activity throughout the ship as sailors scurried about rounding up their personal belongings and stuffing them in their seabags. In ones and twos and groups, the men went to the pier and waited. As they waited, many of them thought about the pain of leaving their familiar old home at sea and wondered about the future.

By 12:15, everyone was present. Ed made a point of talking with those men who were not staying with *Woodside*. There was one man in particular that Ed sought that he seriously wanted to talk with:

"Lieutenant Radcliff—congratulations on your promotion! You have done so much to improve our communications and coordination that I can't thank you enough! And—you fought the ship well when you needed to—good job!"

Prof smiled:

"Thank you, Captain—I have loved every minute I've been aboard!"

Ed paused:

"Actually, Prof—you don't mind if I call you that?"

George grinned:

"No—it's a fine nickname and I don't mind at all."

"Well, Prof—you're headed for ASWORG…"

Prof nodded.

"Did you know about this?"

Radcliff looked grim:

"No, Captain, I had no idea whatsoever! When I received those orders I was shocked—I had no doubt I'd be going to *Woodside Two*!

Ed smiled:

" '*Woodside Two*' ?"

Radcliff smiled:

"Well, some of the fellows have started calling the new ship 'Woodside Two'. It sort of fits…"

Ed laughed:

"But you didn't know about this transfer?"

"No. Although, now that I think back, when I went ASWORG last Tuesday to see my girlfriend, I greeted the head person, Professor Morse. During our brief chat, he asked me if I thought their work was valuable and I agreed it was. He then asked me if I enjoyed being aboard ship and I replied that I did. He seemed thoughtful. I didn't think about it then, but now I wonder if he decided to try to get me transferred there. I don't really know…"

"Well, I hope we'll meet again sometime—good luck!"

"Thanks, Captain—and good luck to you, too."

As they finished their conversation, three long, gray, Navy buses rolled onto the Pier. The men soon piled into their crowded chariots and the trek to Maine began.

Ed couldn't help but look back at "his" ship as the buses pulled away.

*   *   *   *   *   *   *

The first stop was at New York's breathtaking Grand Central Terminal, where the men marched through the concourse and down to their waiting New Haven Railroad train. Joey was amused that the full name of the railroad was the "New York, New Haven, and Hartford Railroad Company". It was no wonder the cars just said "New Haven"!

The enlisted crewmen were seated in two coaches that had been added to Train 24, and the officers were given seats in the Parlor Car. At 3:00 PM sharp, the train began to roll. This was new country for many of the men and they enjoyed watching the Connecticut and Massachusetts scenery pass by. The train rolled into Boston's South Station somewhat later than the advertised 8:25 PM—they clanked to a stop at 9:15.

The next ordeal was getting from South Station to the Boston & Maine Railroad's North Station. Fortunately, whoever planned the trip to get the crew to Maine knew what they were dealing with—there was no easy connection between the stations—so

221

buses had again been arranged. The buses took the men from South Station up to the Boston Navy Yard to be fed, and then back down to North Station. There was plenty of time—the Maine Central train—#55—didn't leave Boston until 1:20 AM. By the time the northbound train pulled out, nearly all the men were propped however they could manage and had gone to sleep.

The train finally pulled slowly to a stop at the lovely brick depot in Bath, Maine at just past noon, Wednesday, June 2. For the men, the station's location could not have been better—Bath Iron Works was an easy march down Water Street and into the shipyard.

The men were housed temporarily in a large barracks used to accommodate crews of recently launched ships. A supervisor from the shipyard announced to the men that there would be a full-crew meeting tomorrow morning to describe the new ship to them. Following the meeting, the men would be arranged into small groups for thorough tours of the ship. The man stated that they would be moving aboard on Friday.

Stu Sigsbee and Ed immediately went in search of someplace to update their uniform markings. The asked the supervisor if there happened to be someplace in town that could do that:

"Aye—go up to Front Street and look for "Downtown Dry Cleaning and Tailors"—they handle that sort of thing all the time."

When told that many of the crew also needed to update their markings, the supervisor smiled:

"I see. Well, I'll call and warn them to expect quite a crowd. The owner is Mr. Allen—he'll be ready for you."

The walk into town was quite pleasant and the quaint downtown was just what one expected of a lovely Maine town. With assistance from a passerby, they found Front Street and quickly spotted "Downtown Dry Cleaning and Tailors". They entered and were greeted by a short, balding man in shirtsleeves with a measuring tape looped around his neck.

When the two visitors entered, the man greeted them:

"Hello, gentlemen. Dick called from the shipyard and told me you'd be coming." He looked puzzled: "I was led to believe there would be quite a crowd..."

Sigsbee smiled:

"Sir, I am quite certain there will be a crowd—and soon! We simply managed to get here before the rest."

"Ah—and what can I do for you?"

Stu and Ed described their new promotions and their need to upgrade their rank insignia. Both men had brought their carry cases (called a "Val-Pak") containing a variety of changes of uniform and all would need attention. Mr. Allen proved to be quite knowledgeable about the requirements. He showed them into a back room and the men were astounded by the vast array of naval uniforms, patches, badges, and insignia that were there.

As they were talking in the backroom, the bell on the front door jangled and many voices could be heard. Mr. Allen went out to greet his new customers and Ed and Sigsbee followed. Ed couldn't help but smile at the dubious faces of his one-time crew. Bill Bevins was standing at the front of the group and he looked concerned.

Ed grinned and spoke:

"Commander Bevins and crew—you are—indeed—at the right place. This is Mr. Allen, the proprietor, and I assure you, you are in VERY good hands!"

Ed turned to Mr. Allen:

"Did I understand you correctly that my friend and I should return here tomorrow morning and our uniforms will be ready?"

"That's right."

"We thank you, sir, and we appreciate your being of such great service to us on such short notice! Thank you!"

The men squeezed aside so Sigsbee and Ed could leave the building.

The meeting the next morning began at 08:30 and Ed and Sigsbee had already retrieved their uniforms. Once the meeting began, Ed found it fascinating. The supervisor was joined by two other men and the meeting started right on time.

The supervisor shared some things that Ed had wondered about:

"Men, welcome to Bath Iron Works, builders of DD-632. We have a saying around here: 'Bath Built is Best Built". We are very serious about that. We want every ship we build to be well-constructed, strong, and able to accomplish its mission. You are taking over a very fine ship and we wish you great success against our enemies!"

"There is something rather unique about 632: when she was launched 2 ½ months ago, she was not christened. The Navy Department had explained about the greatly successful history of your previous ship and explained that that ship would soon be decommissioned and this ship would then be commissioned to bear her name. As a result, the commissioning ceremony—scheduled for noon, Wednesday, June 9—will be a bit different from normal. Now that your old ship has been decommissioned, the name is available for this ship, so our ceremony will include an abbreviated christening prior to the commissioning."

Ed was fascinated.

"I understand your former commanding officer is present here?"

Ed raised his hand.

"The christening ceremony will be conducted here at pier-side. The daughter of the Chairman of our Board of Selectmen will perform the christening with the assistance of your former captain." He looked at Ed and smiled. Ed was deeply touched.

The supervisor then began a detailed description of the new Fletcher-class destroyer with reference to a large cut-away drawing of the ship. After lunch, Sigsbee, Ed, and Lieutenant-Commander Bevins received a personally guided tour of the new ship. The first thing Ed noticed was that the ship still smelled like fresh paint. The next thing was the amazing array of modern weapons and weapon systems. From the latest radios to the latest radar, to the latest sonar, DD-632 had it all. And the number of guns of various calibers was breathtaking. DD-632 was much larger than DD-203 had been and could steam much farther. Ed felt serious regret that he was not taking the new ship to sea.

Following the special tour, the crew began their orientation to the new ship. As they toured, it was explained that divisions would not be bunking together—the thought was that you didn't, for example, want to lose all your electricians in a single attack. Mike and Joey smiled at the thought and they quickly selected bunks in the same berthing compartment, just forward of the mess deck. For both of them, their new equipment meant a lot to learn—quickly!

Moving aboard on Friday was chaotic—the men were still trying to find their way about the ship and lugging a heavy seabag didn't help speed things.

As the crew was getting oriented, so were the officers, and—due to the promotions and transfers, there were some changes. As now-skipper Bill Bevins studied the list, he noted a possible move that would better utilize his staff. He called Carl Bascom to the new Captain's Cabin, located on the Main Deck level next to the new "Combat Information Center".

"Carl, since Commander Palmer is gone and I've been bumped up, that leaves us needing an XO. I know you are our Navigator, and I appreciate the fine work you do—he grinned, "—we haven't lost our way yet!"

Bascom smiled.

"But, Carl, I've learned that many ships like this do not have a separate Navigator and a separate XO—they combine the two into one position. That seems to make sense—there isn't usually as much XO work at sea and there isn't usually much navigator work in port. As a result, the combination seems to work. What do you think?"

Bascom was thoughtful:

"Well, Bill, you might be right—and I'd rather not have to break in a stranger as XO. Let's give it a try!"

DD-632 was a beehive of activity as men found their way around and began to learn the intricacies of their new assignments. In addition, nearly 100 new men were expected to join the ship on Monday, so completing the "Watch, Quarter, and Station Bill" was complex. In addition, there were the details of the christening and commissioning ceremonies to be finalized. Bevins tried to stay on top of it all...

Being the CO is more complicated than I thought! He laughed to himself: *Where is Captain Palmer when I need him??*

It turned out that Captain Ed Palmer was near at hand and he recognized the complexities facing Bill Bevins. Ed "happened" to wander aboard on Monday morning and he "happened" to check in with Bevins—and to offer his assistance if needed. His assistance was gratefully accepted!

Wednesday
June 9, 1943
Bath Iron Works

The ceremonies were scheduled to begin at 14:00. DD-632 had been bustling virtually night and day since the crew moved aboard Friday and especially since the new men arrived on Monday. The ship's officers had teamed up to get the men properly assigned and properly berthed. Each division had then begun diligent orientation and training for all hands. They had an exceptionally short time to get the crew ready, but the theory was that, since *Woodside's* men were well acquainted with each other and with their duties, it wouldn't take much time to adapt to the new ship. It turned out to be a bad assumption—DD-632 was a vastly different ship from DD-203.

Joey found that the new Model QJB sonar unit was different from his old one, but Wirtz gathered the operators and quickly brought them up to speed. The biggest difference wasn't so much the unit, as the location—the sound machine was located at the rear of the pilothouse rather than in some sort of Ops Center. Joey and his mates had become accustomed to DD-203's common location for sonar, radar, and radio repeaters. The new ship did not have a centralized "Ops Center" but, rather, had a new space called the "Combat Information Center" that correlated all of the necessary combat information and data. The scanning equipment was not located there, however, but was scattered about the ship—again, as a means of protecting from loss of all systems at once due to a single battle damage. With a modern sound-powered telephone system, the information could flow quickly regardless of physical location.

If Joey's new station was fairly recognizable, Mike's situation was dramatically different. The new *Woodside* had a scale of armament that dwarfed that of the old ship: Beginning with five 5"/38 Mk 30 enclosed main guns, to ten 40MM barrels, and seven 20MM guns. It made Mike's lone quad 40MM from the old days look positively anemic! LTJG Shulman and Chief Landis were the recipients of the majority of the new men because they were needed to man the new guns. For example, each of the new 5"/38 turrets typically required up to ten men in the turret itself and additional 7-10 men in the ammunition handling room. The guns were controlled by a Mark 37 Gun Fire Control System that, hopefully, meant the days of Mike and the other gunners manually aiming and firing were relegated to the past.

Despite the exigencies of learning the new ship, she first had to formally join the fleet.

Sigsbee and Ed were visiting with Lieutenant Commander Bevins while awaiting the commencement of the ceremonies. As 14:00 approached, several visitors came aboard, including some of the plant leaders and a variety of civilians from the town. Ed was introduced to Rebecca, the young lady who would conduct the christening. Her official title was "Sponsor" and Ed was amused to learn that her qualification for that august post was that she was the Principal of the Woodside School in nearby Topsham. At 13:45, everyone left the ship and the crew—wearing Dress Whites, was lined up on the pier. In addition to the expected speaker's platform, a platform had ingeniously been built that cantilevered from the pier to just ahead of the ship's bow where Rebecca, with Ed's assistance, would christen the ship by breaking the traditional bottle of champagne on the bow. Ed hoped they wouldn't end up swimming.

It turned out that Rear Admiral Sigsbee would be the Master of Ceremonies and that Ed would make the formal commissioning statement. But first, the christening—

Woodside was decked out in red, white, and blue bunting and the speaker's and christening platforms were also draped accordingly. It looked very festive.

At precisely 14:00, Admiral Sigsbee called the group to order. He briefly described the order of events and then turned the speaker's platform over to one of the City Selectmen, who spoke rather droningly for several minutes. He was followed by the Director of the Works who, thankfully, spoke briefly and energetically. Several other yard people spoke until finally, it was time for Sigsbee to introduce the christening.

Sigsbee began with a heartfelt tribute to the "old" *Woodside*, commenting on her exemplary war service and numerous successes in helping to tame the U-boat menace in the North Atlantic. He then explained the rather unusual circumstances that led to the ceremony about to occur. With that, he turned and announced:

"Would the sponsor of USS WOODSIDE (DD-632) please bestow upon this ship her formal name and christen her accordingly!"

Rebecca turned nervously and took the bottle from Ed and—under her breath exclaimed to him:

"I sure hope this breaks like it's supposed to!"

She then stepped forward and stated loudly:

"I hereby christen thee United States Ship Woodside! Go with God!"

She stepped to the front of the platform, pulled the bottle back and then swung it hard against the reinforced steel bow of the ship.

The glass shattered, spraying her and Ed—and *Woodside*—with Champagne. The crowd broke into applause, the crew cheered, and photos were taken. Rebecca and Ed stepped gratefully back onto solid ground and joined the others on the speaker's stand.

Sigsbee then continued:

"It is now time for USS *Woodside* to join her sisters of the fleet in serving our nation. Captain Palmer, would you issue the order please!"

Ed stepped to the microphone:

"Would the prospective Commanding Officer of USS *Woodside* please come forward?" Bevins marched forward and stood at attention in front of Ed. "Sir, I hereby order you to place this gallant ship into commission."

Lieutenant Commander Bevins stepped to the microphone:

"It is my honor to order the prospective Executive Officer of USS *Woodside* to hoist the national colors and raise the commissioning pennant!"

Lieutenant Bascom was prepared and the colors and the long, thin, commissioning pennant unfurled and rose smoothly to the top of the mast.

Bill Bevins then read his orders appointing him Commanding Officer of the new ship. Following that, he issued his order:

"Executive Officer—set the watch!"

The men remained in ranks awaiting the most time-honored part of the ceremony:

The ship's sponsor—Rebecca—came to the microphone and stated loudly:

"Man our ship and bring her to life!"

The crew responded, "Aye, aye, Ma'am!" The crew then broke ranks and ran to the brow and onto the ship as the band played "Anchors Aweigh!" The crew manned the rails as the radar antennae began turning and various other systems began to move—signifying that the ship had "come to life".

USS *Woodside* (DD-632) was now a formal part of the United States Navy.

Thursday
June 10, 1943
Bath, Maine

Following the ceremony, Sigsbee and Ed remained at the side of the ship and shared conversation with the various attendees. It was all very nice and very affirming, but it also served to make Ed even more despondent about heading for a shore job. Eventually, everyone slowly drifted away but Ed had moved away to lean with one foot on one of the mooring bollards and gaze at the new ship. After a while, Stu Sigsbee approached him and asked gently:

"Still wishing she was yours?"

Ed jumped—he hadn't heard Sigsbee approach. He looked embarrassed:

"Yes, I suppose so. She's a fine vessel and I know the old crew is great—I just feel let down. I am a reasonably good seagoing commander, but I know nothing about the rocks and shoals of Washington. This new assignment is rather intimidating…"

"Do you want to take a few days' leave before reporting?"

"No. I considered that, but I have no one to see and nowhere to go. I may as well just get to Washington and try to get settled there. How about you—are you going to spend some time with Suzanne?"

Sigsbee shook his head:

"No—we've had a lot of time together while I've been in Newport. She's going to stay in our house there and—like you—I want to get to Washington and get started."

Ed looked forlorn:

"Stu—you're going to have to really hold my hand in Washington!"

Sigsbee laughed:

"Ha! No one has ever had to hold your hand for anything! Relax—you'll soon be telling the cocktail circuit how to win the war—and I'll be right beside you agreeing with every word you say!"

Ed smiled:

"Thanks, ol' buddy—I'll do my best to be your right-hand man!"

"Well, Mr. Right Hand—let's go find a nice dinner!"

The men did, indeed, find a nice dinner at a cozy restaurant downtown. Over after-dinner coffee, Ed mused:

"Boy, this is sure a long ways from being shot at by U-boats!"

Stu just chuckled.

* * * * * * *

The next morning, "Mr. Right Hand Man" went to work on getting them from Bath to Washington. It wasn't easy. Because they had not yet assumed their new positions, they had very low travel priorities—only AA level. There were no military flights from Bath to anywhere and the nearest Navy facility was in Boston, 150 miles away. Even getting to Boston wouldn't help much with their low priorities, so it obviously would require a wearying train ride all the way to Washington. After breakfast, Ed went to the depot and huddled with the ticket agent.

The man's first words weren't encouraging:

"Well—it seems like everyone's trying to get to Washington…"

After a long and detailed consultation of a huge book entitled "The Official Guide to the Railways", an itinerary was developed that would take them to Boston via the Maine Central Railroad's train #54, leaving Bath at 2:55 PM. They would arrive in Boston at 6:20 PM, but the next leg wasn't until the next morning, so a hotel was booked for the night. The next day, they would board the New Haven's train #177—named "The Senator"—for an 11:00 AM departure. In New York City, the train would change from the New Haven to the Pennsylvania Railroad, but the train, itself, would continue to Washington, arriving at 8:20 PM. At least—that was the plan…

Current travel restrictions required at least one week's advance notice before booking rail travel. The agent was understanding, however, and—because of Sigsbee's flag rank—he overlooked the rule and booked the men for departure that very afternoon—Thursday, June 10. It was surprising there was room for them.

The men packed their bags and were waiting on the station platform by 2:30. They needn't have hurried—the train clanked and squealed to a stop ten minutes late. The door to the car before them opened and the conductor climbed down and placed the step stool. Two rather matronly women alighted, gracing Stu and Ed with a nod. The conductor then indicated they should board—and he offered these words of encouragement:

"Good luck, men!"

They climbed the steps and turned through the vestibule into the coach—and into bedlam. There had been seven stops before Bath and the train was well—VERY well—patronized. All seats were full, babies were crying, and people were sitting on chair arms or on their luggage. The conductor followed them in:

"Don't get your hopes up—the other cars are just like this."

It was going to be a long three hours to Boston!

If the conductor hadn't taken pity on them because of Stu's exalted rank, they would have stood all the way. The man's thoughtfulness allowed them to perch in his "office"—a stool set before a fold-down shelf behind the last row of seats. It was better than standing.

*　*　*　*　*　*　*

When they finally reached Boston—nearly an hour late, there turned out to be great compensation. They had been booked into the Bostonian Hotel—one of the finest in the city. Stu was glad their travel voucher would cover the cost! They took a taxi to the hotel and were treated like royalty after that—Boston knew the Navy because of the huge Navy Yard and they understood rank—being an Admiral meant something in Boston! The first of the amenities Ed sought was the large, lovely shower!

It was nearly 8 PM when they entered the luxurious dining room. The evening rush was over, but the room was still crowded. They were quickly ushered to a table, offered wine, and given a menu. Rationing was certainly in effect, but the menu was surprisingly varied. They ordered and sat back to await the arrival of the food.

The sumptuous meal arrived and both men enjoyed it thoroughly. Once they had finished, they sat back and relaxed. They were sharing comments on the ordeal of their train ride when a naval Lieutenant Commander approached them:

"Admiral—Captain—forgive me for interrupting. My friends and I are at the next table and we couldn't help but overhear of your railroad ordeal. We've experienced that, too, and so we are hoping you will allow us to buy you a drink as a small compensation for your troubles."

Stu smiled:

"Why, Commander—that is a most generous offer and we gratefully accept. Thank you!"

Stu looked to their table and saw two other naval officers and three prosperous-looking women. He raised his glass to salute them.

The Commander hesitated, then:

"Gentlemen, if you've no other plans, why don't you slip over to our table and join us?"

Stu looked at Ed, shrugged, and answered:

"Why, that's very kind of you—we will. Thank you!"

Stu left money to cover their bill and they moved to join their neighbors. Introductions were made. The Lieutenant Commander spoke:

"Gentlemen, my name is Frank Overton and this is my wife, Lucille." He then pointed to one of the Lieutenants: "This fellow is my nephew, Allan Destin and his wife, Carol. And this is Ralph Gordon and his girlfriend, Sandra."

Stu introduced himself and Ed.

Commander Overton then explained:

"We're here in these sumptuous surroundings to celebrate my return to shore duty—I'm the new Engineering Officer at the Navy Yard. Al and Ralph are here temporarily as their ship is upgraded."

Stu explained about his and Ed's orders to Washington. Following that, the conversation flowed freely and everyone had an enjoyable evening. The group finally parted a little after 10 PM. Commander Overton said goodbye and added:

"Well, gentlemen, it has been a pleasure meeting you. Who knows—we may meet again sometime..." It was a prescient statement.

*   *   *   *   *   *   *

On Saturday morning, New Haven train #177—The Senator—pulled out at 11:00 AM sharp. Stu and Ed were comfortably ensconced in seats in the Parlor Car, far from the crowding in the coaches. Just before the train began to glide out of the station, a middle-aged couple entered the car and took the two seats on the other side of Ed. He glanced up and smiled a welcome, then returned to watching as Boston rolled past. An hour later, as the train stopped in Providence, the woman turned to Ed and asked:

"Excuse me, but are you attached to the Navy in Boston?"

Ed smiled:

"No, Ma'am, I'm on my way to Washington to a new assignment."

She smiled and glanced at her husband:

"We are traveling to Washington, also—my husband is what they are calling a 'Dollar-a-Year Man'."

Ed looked blank.

"You've not heard that term?"

"No. I've been at sea a great deal, so there are many recent things ashore that I haven't encountered yet."

She looked proudly at her husband, and then turned back to Ed:

"Well, you see, certain prominent businessmen—such as my husband—have agreed to go to Washington and run important offices for the wage of one dollar per year. It's our patriotic duty to help out."

Ed nodded:

"And what is it your husband does?"

"He'll be at the 'Civilian Scientific Council.'"

Ed looked blank.

"It's an important appointment..."

Ed nodded: "I'm sure it is."

She looked a bit befuddled—as though her pronouncement was not greeted with sufficient awe. Her husband smiled and leaned across his wife to speak with Ed:

"My wife," he said with a chuckle, "is proud of her husband."

Ed smiled and responded:

"...And that's a good thing for a wife to be!"

They went on to talk of his "actual" position as Director of Science at a large chemical company based in Boston with huge plants located all across the country. He explained how some of his peers felt his knowledge might be helpful to the war effort, and so he volunteered his services to the government. He then began asking Ed questions regarding his naval experiences and the conversation went smoothly from there. Ed learned they were Edith and Stanley Stillman and they, along with Stu Sigsbee and Ed, enjoyed a nice lunch together in the dining car. Back in the Parlor Car, Edith dozed off, and Ed and Stu talked quietly about what might await them in Washington.

Arrival at Pennsylvania Station in New York City was an amazing experience—Ed now witnessed the definition of "mayhem" first hand. A large number of the passengers from Boston left the train in New York, to be replaced by an even larger contingent of passengers boarding to go to Washington. The flood of arriving passengers collided with the flood of departing passengers on the platform and things looked truly chaotic. Ed commented on it to Stu:

"Well, Ed, the guy at the gate is supposed to wait until all of the passengers getting off go out the gate, and then let the new ones in. Obviously, something went wrong—who knows, maybe they just flooded right past him and ignored him..."

Finally, the mob diminished and, a few minutes later than the advertised 4:30 PM, the train slid out of the station and headed for Washington. Watching the front of the train, Ed saw a new locomotive had been attached—a Tuscan Red, streamlined electric locomotive with "Pennsylvania" lettered on its side. He noted the ride was especially smooth.

Soon after departure, a large, florid-faced man in a gray suit entered the car and passed by Ed and the Stillmans. As he passed, he looked at Mr. Stillman and grunted:

"Stillman."

Stillman replied:

"Collins."

After the man passed, Edith whispered to her husband:

"It's that horrid Bill Collins! What does HE want? Always acting holier-than-thou and thinking he's better than anyone else!"

Stanley 'shushed' her:

"Now, Edith, you know he thinks he's a big shot in Washington…"

Ed was beginning to learn that service in the nation's capitol might not be as straightforward as commanding a warship.

The ride continued with quiet conversation in the parlor car as Ed watched the scenery streaking past—this was a FAST train!

They finally arrived at Washington's beautiful Union Station right on time—quite a feat, given the enormous wartime rail traffic. Several other trains were arriving or departing at about the same time and the unbelievable rush on the platform was nothing compared to the jam-up in the main concourse. Ed and Stu found it not only difficult to move ahead, but even difficult to remain together!

 Once they finally pushed, climbed, dodged, and shouldered their way to the exit, the next problem occurred:

"Stu, do we have someplace to stay?"

Sigsbee grimaced:

"Ed, this city is filled to overflowing and places to stay are very, very hard to find. Suzanne gave me the name of one of her friends who lives here and said I should call her when we arrived—maybe she could help us. I noticed, however, that even the phone booths here are jammed with people, so I suggest we try to get a cab and find a phone at a drugstore or something. Maybe we should even go to Main Navy and see what happens there…"

Ed thought about it:

"Hmm. It's Saturday night—maybe Main Navy would be a good idea. It's probably less crowded on a weekend night and we might be ahead to try there."

They agreed and, after nearly twenty minutes of standing in front of the station frantically flagging a cab, they were successful.

On their approach to the huge building, they were, as usual, impressed with its size. A closer look, however, showed how worn out and beat up the place was—obviously worse than the last time they had been here a year ago. They paid the cab and entered, encountering a desk manned by a Chief Petty Officer.

Stu took the lead:

"Good evening, Chief. We're reporting here on Monday for duty, but I'm wondering if you have a telephone we could use?"

The Chief looked stern:

"Why do you need a phone—uh—Admiral?"

"Well, Chief, if we can't find anywhere to stay, we'll just have to camp out right here in your lobby…"

243

The Chief didn't seem to appreciate Stu's attempt at humor, but he hooked his thumb toward two telephone booths in the far rear corner. Stu finally managed to connect with Suzanne's friend:

"Hello, Charlene, this is Stu Sigsbee—I think Suzanne might have told you I'd be calling?"

(Pause)

"Yes, we just arrived and managed to get a cab to Main Navy. What? No, we have no idea where to stay—all of the Navy lodging is full with long waiting lines."

(Pause)

"Yes, Charlene, there are two of us—me and my assistant, Captain Palmer. Hmm, I can imagine! Can you suggest anything?"

(Pause)

"Why, Charlene, that would be wonderful! Outside? Yes, we'll be waiting. Thank you!"

Sigsbee explained:

"Suzanne had telephoned her and she says she tried all over the city to find a hotel, or an apartment, or even a garage for rent that we might get—but there's nothing. Her husband is going to drive over here and pick us up and take us to their house where we can discuss the problem."

Half an hour later, a blue Chevrolet sedan pulled to the curb and the gray-haired man inside called them to enter. They did:

"Hello, Stu—long time, no see!"

"Hello, Walt—it has been a while! We certainly appreciate your coming to get us…"

Walt laughed:

"Well, the way this city is now, there's no knowing what might have happened to you fellows if you were stuck out here all night!"

The drive out to Woodley Park was pleasant, but Ed was beginning to feel the effects of their very long day and arrival at Walt and Charlene Gregor's lovely home was a relief. They were warmly welcomed, given a cool drink and all sat down to solve the housing problem. After much discussion, it was decided that Stu and Ed would stay with the Gregors' for a couple of days until the men could learn what the Navy had in mind for them.

Monday
June 14, 1943
Main Navy

A restful sleep both Saturday and Sunday night helped to fortify Stu and Ed for whatever awaited them in town. Walt generously dropped them off at Main Navy on his way to his office downtown on M Street. They entered and found another Chief—this one slightly less caustic and slightly more helpful.

"Good Morning Admiral, Captain," he said, "how may I help you?"

Stu explained about their orders and handed over the sheaf of papers. The Chief read them carefully, then:

"Gentlemen, if you will wait a few moments, I'll notify your command that you have arrived."

They waited quite a while until a rather mousy-looking Lieutenant came through a door in the rear of the lobby and approached them:

"Admiral—Captain, please follow me."

Hmm, noted Ed, *no greeting, no welcome, nothing—just "follow me"! Hmm...*

He led them through a labyrinthine maze that soon had Ed lost. The Navy Department Building—commonly referred to as "Main Navy"—consisted of a huge building of three stories with nine parallel wings. They marched along forever until finally, at a column post numbered "7", they turned right into one of the wings. They hiked all the way to the end of the wing and turned right to a door with a sign 1797 posted next to it. The Lieutenant opened the door and indicated the men should enter. What they found was a very small room containing one, small, well-dented metal desk and one four-drawer, well-dented file cabinet. The Lieutenant turned to go…

Rear Admiral Stuart Sigsbee, USN, got a look on his face that looked as though he'd bitten a hot pepper. He spoke sharply:

"Lieutenant! Return here, please!"

The man turned and came back with a questioning look.

"Lieutenant—what is this? This—closet? Just what are we doing here?"

The Lieutenant shaded red:

"Admiral—this is your office."

"Office?!" Sigsbee exploded. "Office? This is a closet! Are the two of us expected to function effectively in here?" He was loud on purpose. "No! This is not acceptable! In fact, this is an insult!"

The young man stammered:

"Uh—well—I—uh—"

"Who assigned this…"

Stu was in mid-sentence when Ed pointed to the faded paint of a previous sign for the room—it could be read saying "Janitor's Closet".

"…this JANITOR'S Closet?!"

"Uh, Sir, I was directed to bring you here by someone in Admiral Low's office."

Sigsbee stared at the fellow:

"Then you just lead us right back out of this janitor's closet and take us to whoever dreamed up this insulting nightmare! Let's go!"

So back they went out of the wing and down through what everyone called "the headhouse". They climbed some well-worn stairs to the second floor and hiked to wing #4. They finally entered a large office filled with woman typists pounding a cacophony on their many typewriters. They went to a door where the Lieutenant knocked and entered. They followed and found a Lieutenant Commander sitting at a desk piled with papers and a jangling telephone. He looked up sharply and seemed surprised to see an Admiral in his office. He sat there.

Sigsbee was in no mood for any more nonsense:

"Commander—you come to attention when a superior officer enters!"

The man fumbled, stood from his chair, and came to a position somewhat resembling attention.

"Commander—are you responsible for the assignment of office quarters for me and my staff?"

"Yes."

Sharply: "'Yes' what?!"

"Yes, sir."

"Commander, are you at all familiar with space 1797?"

"Sir, that space is shown on our records as an office space."

"Have you personally inspected space 1797?"

After a hesitation: "No, sir, I have not."

"So you are not aware that space 1797 is a janitor's closet?"

"What? That's impossible!"

"That does it! You imply that I am lying—Commander, come with me—we're going for a little lesson in doing your job properly."

Sigsbee led the group at a march out through the busy office, down the halls, down the stairs and all the way to space 1797—previously identified as "Janitor's Closet". Their passage through the building attracted a fair amount of attention—and even a smile or two.

"Commander—please read that sign out loud."

"1797."

"And read this sign out loud."

" 'Janitor's Closet'."

"Commander, do you agree that I am telling you the truth when I describe this little box as a "janitor's closet'?"

"Yes, sir. No offense, Admiral."

Sigsbee made a show of taking a deep breath:

"Commander—assigning an Admiral to a janitor's closet for an office is an insult. And then implying that Admiral is lying when he describes it to you is also insulting. Commander, we are not starting off on a right foot! Now, why don't we head back to your—spacious—office and rectify all this?"

 The Lieutenant Commander—his name was Booth—led them into his office and had them sit down. He picked up the telephone and dialed a number from memory:

"Hello—it's Booth. Is he available? Yes, it's important."

He hung up the phone and *respectfully* asked the men to accompany him. They went around a couple of corners to another office with the nameplate "Capt. Fitz". Booth knocked and they were invited in. As an Admiral entered the office, Fitz immediately started to pop up to attention:

Sigsbee looked sternly at Booth, then stated: "Captain, as you were. We're here for your assistance in rectifying what appears to be several mistakes."

"Thank you, Admiral. I don't believe I've had the pleasure of meeting the Admiral…"

Stu reached across and shook Fitz hand:

"Sigsbee—Stuart Sigsbee. I and my assistant, Captain Palmer, have been ordered here to Tenth Fleet."

"Ordered? Sir, I am not aware of any such orders." He hastily added: "I'm not questioning your word, sir, but I'm a bit confused…"

Sigsbee grimaced:

"There seems to be a lot of that around here. Perhaps these will help…" He handed Fitz a copy of his and Ed's orders. Fitz read them carefully.

"Admiral Sigsbee, I apologize for my ignorance in this matter—I have received no information regarding your assignment here. Perhaps something was said when you met Admiral Low?"

Sigsbee gave a small smile:

"Captain, I haven't see Frog Low since we served together on New Mexico—a long time ago."

"Oh, my! That would seem to be the beginning of the problem— you should have been taken to meet Admiral Low immediately upon your arrival here. I am certain he will clarify all of this confusion. Let me make a call…"

Captain Fitz made the call, then invited Stu and Ed to join him to go meet Admiral Low. They entered the busy office and walked to the rear where a lieutenant was acting as Executive Secretary for the Admiral. He opened the door and announced them. Sigsbee led:

"Well, Stu Sigsbee! How long has it been?"

"Hello, Francis—I think since we served on *New Mexico...*"

"There's been a lot of water over a lot of dams since those dim ages! So what can I do for you?"

Stu looked dismayed and Captain Fitz was quick to speak:

"Admiral, Admiral Sigsbee and Captain Palmer have been ordered here to Tenth Fleet."

Low looked surprised:

"Ordered here? I've not heard anything about such orders!"

Sigsbee held out their sheaf of papers:

"If the Admiral would be so kind..."

Low read them carefully:

"Stu—I'm sorry! I'm supposed to be in charge here and I have no knowledge of this at all!"

Sigsbee was dismayed:

"Admiral Low, I have no idea about any of this—those are our properly endorsed orders. If you didn't request us, I can't imagine..."

He stopped in mid-sentence:

"Uh, actually, something has just occurred to me. Several months ago, I was visited in my office in Newport by Admiral Horace Cuthbert from the Officer Placement Bureau. He was insistent that Captain Palmer be brought ashore and placed in a position that would have been little more than a clerk job. You will remember that Captain Palmer's ship is responsible for sinking at least eight U-boats and damaging many others? The proposal struck me as a massive waste of talent and I said so to Admiral Cuthbert. In fact, I protested strongly. I wonder…"

Low grimaced:

"I think you're onto something, Stu. We had placed a call for submarine expert officers to serve in our Operations Section which is now a part of our Combat Intelligence Section. It sounds like Cuthbert took that to heart and found out about you, Captain Palmer." He paused: "Stu, how did your talk go with Cuthbert?"

Sigsbee grimaced:

"Frankly, it didn't go well and our parting was rather strained."

Low nodded:

"It sounds like Admiral Horace Cuthbert has managed to have the last laugh, doesn't it?"

Sigsbee shook his head ruefully:

"What can we do about it?"

Low shook his head:

"In actuality—nothing. Cuthbert will claim he is just responding to our request. Sorry, Stu."

After a few moments, Stu asked:

"Well, Admiral—now what? New orders to take us someplace else?"

Low was thoughtful:

"Stu, now that I think about it—no—I think we'll keep you right here and thank our lucky stars you fellows showed up. I don't have a complete idea yet, but I'll give it some thought and make some calls. In the meantime, did they give you an office?"

Sigsbee swallowed hard before responding. He then went into painful detail about the fiasco about the janitor's closet.

"Stu, I'll look into that. Why don't you gentlemen spend today getting settled into Washington and let's meet here again tomorrow at—say—14:00?"

It was agreed and Stu and Ed left. Captain Fitz remained behind for a few moments, then returned to his office calling firmly for Lieutenant Commander Booth to come to his office immediately.

For Stu and Ed, Monday had been a very busy day—and it was still morning.

"Ed, let's stop by our friendly Chief at the desk and ask about lodging." They did and received a recommendation of who to see that might help them…

They followed a familiar path and were back in front of Commander Booth's desk when he returned from Captain Fitz' office looking abashed. His expression when he saw Stu and Ed awaiting him was mostly one of embarrassment.

"Hello, again, Commander."

Booth looked serious as he spoke:

"Admiral—Captain, I offer my humblest apologies to you both. As you know, we had no information that you had been assigned here and we didn't know anything about you. I was told to assign you an office, so I looked down our list of available spaces and gave you the first available space. Obviously, that was a major error on my part. I hope you will accept my sincere apology—no offense was intended, I assure you."

Stu looked levelly at him:

"Commander, this entire situation is inexcusable—but it is not your fault. We certainly accept your apology." He paused: "Now, if we might move in a different direction—what can you suggest for lodging for us? Might there be something at the Washington Navy Yard?"

Booth's relief at the acceptance of his apology was immediately replaced by a feeling of helplessness:

"Admiral, I don't know what to say. I wish dearly that I could help you, but housing in this city is virtually impossible to find. I will, of course, telephone the Navy Yard and inquire, but my last call to them a few days ago was futile."

He picked up his phone and dialed. When answered, he requested to speak with a Captain Jacobson. Booth explained the issue and almost pleaded for assistance, reminding the Captain that this request regarded an Admiral's needs—it didn't work.

He hung up the phone and held his hands in a helpless gesture:

"Gentlemen, I am truly sorry. The Navy Yard has very limited housing available and it has been fully filled for quite some time." He thought for a moment: "Perhaps we can get lucky in another way: there are private families around the city who are renting spare bedrooms as lodging—maybe we can find something like that…"

Stu looked at Ed and shrugged:

"Commander, we might already have a lead in that direction through a friend of my wife who lives here. May I use your phone?"

Stu spoke with Charlene Gregor and explained the situation. She was thoughtful, but stated she would have Walt swing by Main Navy at lunchtime and bring them back out to the house— she said she had an idea.

As the fellows stood outside awaiting Walt's arrival, they had a great view of the hordes of people jamming the sidewalks at lunchtime. Ed noticed that a great many were women—many of them rather attractive. Stu noticed, too:

"Well, Ed, here you are—a single man in a city full of women—how about that?"

Ed just chuckled. Sigsbee turned serious:

"Ed, do you ever hear from Lorena or your kids?"

Ed was saddened:

"No, Stu—never a word. When her Father's office drew up the divorce decree, the agreement was that I would never have to pay alimony or child support, but the tradeoff was that I would not have visitation rights and I am not allowed to seek any contact with any of them. I was completely erased from their lives. That sad chapter ended a long time ago..."

"Sorry, Ed."

Shortly, Walt's now-familiar Chevy sedan pulled to the curb and they were soon on their way back to the lovely and restful climes of Woodley Park.

Following a delightful lunch taken on the patio, Charlene explained her idea:

"Stuart, I'm not a bit surprised about your difficulty in finding housing—Washington started filling up right after the war started and has continued to fill since then. But here's what I can offer you and Edwin: the room you now staying in is available for one of you, and I called my friend Mary French over on Garfield Terrace. She and Phil have an extra room over their garage that they don't really use and it's become full of stuff. She said they could empty it out and it would make a nice bedroom—it even has a small bathroom—and you could take meals with them in the main house. She said they'd charge $25 per month."

Stu looked at Ed. It was certainly not what Ed expected—he thought he'd just rent an apartment and be ready to go. That was obviously impossible, though, and this situation seemed to meet their needs:

"Well, Stu, it sounds like this might be the perfect solution all around. It works for me."

Sigsbee nodded.

Charlene interjected:

"Before we decide, we should probably run over there and see what the room is like."

Arrival at the French residence showed a beautiful home set back slightly from the street with a small, well-tended front lawn. The detached garage was set back from the house and had an external staircase to the upstairs room. They heard noises from the garage and found Mary wrestling with a large box of old belongings. Introductions were made and they all hiked upstairs. The room turned out to be rather large and did, indeed, include a fully functional bathroom with a shower. And the room was full of stuff.

Mary explained:

"It will take a few hours to get this junk out of here and probably another day or two to get it painted. After that, we have a spare bed and a couple of chairs we can move in and that should serve. I'll be on the lookout for a small table…"

The only decision remaining was "which man goes to which room"?

Sigsbee spoke:

"Ed, it seems to make sense for me to stay with Walt and Charlene because we're old friends. Would you be comfortable joining the Frenches?"

Ed smiled at Mary:

"If the Frenches will have me, I'd love to bunk here."

Tuesday
June 15, 1943
14:00
Main Navy

Admiral Sigsbee and Captain Palmer had an enlightening talk while they waited for their meeting with Admiral Low.

"Ed, I hope you don't think I'm being petty about this office assignment thing—here in Washington, status is granted by things other than rank or skill. Appearances matter. Whether a flag officer has a car, and the size and the make of the car, are vitally important. If that officer has a driver—is the driver enlisted or an officer? Obviously an officer-level driver imparts greater status. The location of one's office within a building is crucial, as are the size of the office and the size of the office staff. Et Cetera, Et Cetera. Unfortunately, if we intend to actually achieve anything here, we have to grab all the status possible in order to be taken seriously."

Ed just shook his head sadly:

"Why am I not in command of a ship of war? I don't belong here!"

"Don't worry—you'll do fine. Besides, we came here to shake up the 'cocktail circuit', not to join it!'

At the stroke of 14:00, they were ushered into Admiral Low's office.

Once they were all seated, Stu first described their new living arrangements and the Admiral was happy to hear that problem was solved. Then the Admiral began:

"Stu, the more I've thought about your surprise arrival here, the more I think it's propitious. Nearly everyone working at Tenth Fleet is a landlubber—even most of the officers are long away from sea duty. These people, however, are excellent at the work they do and they are already making a big difference in our conduct of anti-submarine efforts. What you and Captain Palmer can do is bring us a dose of practical reality.

"Before I go more into what I have in mind for you, I'd like to describe how we're structured: We are composed of five primary sections: Operations, Anti-submarine Measures, Convoy and Routing, the Civilian Scientific Council, and the Air Anti-submarine Development Unit. We also work very closely with the Anti-Submarine Warfare Operational Research Group—which we call 'ASWORG'—that provides regular reports of new technologies and tactics to us.

"The Operations Section, under Captain Haines, pulls together all our sources of intelligence to guide the operations of the various Hunter-Killer Groups. They recently scored a great success: on May 22, the USS *Bogue* group tracked down and destroyed U-569—*Bogue's* first confirmed kill."

On hearing the news, Ed and Stu looked at each other and smiled. Admiral Low noticed:

"Gentlemen, am I missing something?"

"No, Admiral—it's just that Ed's boat, *Woodside*, trained with *Bogue's* group when it was first established."

"Ah. Well, to continue: The Anti-Submarine Measures section, led by Captain Fitz, whom you've met, is divided into Air and Surface sections. They are responsible for the correlation of ASW research, materiel development, and training and disseminating that information to the forces afloat.

"The Convoy and Routing section, known as 'C&R', is led by Rear Admiral Martin Metcalf and is responsible for tracking the U.S. portion of convoys and planning the routes they take across the Atlantic. They maintain massive wall charts detailing all ongoing convoy operations in the Atlantic. Intelligence received by the Operations Branch, once sanitized, is also added to update these charts."

Ed nodded: "Like those of Commander Winn in Liverpool..."

"Yes," Admiral Low added, "Commander Kenneth Knowles leads the Atlantic Ocean section and he worked closely with Winn to develop what has now become our C&R."

Sigsbee added: "Ed and *Woodside* were deeply involved with those early efforts."

"Another good reason to keep you here!"

"Well—continuing: that takes us to our last element, the Civilian Scientific Council. These are civilian scientists dedicated to developing advanced methods to conduct our anti-submarine warfare. They do a great deal of theoretical work and ASWORG is a portion of this group."

Stu and Ed nodded—Tenth Fleet was a complex entity.

"So, gentlemen," Low continued, "the obvious question is: 'Where do you fit in?' I've given a great deal of thought to that…"

Both Stu and Ed were eager to hear…

"Gentlemen, the people we have here, and those who lead them, are doing a marvelous job. Replacing any of them is not an option and I do not see such a role for you. What I do see is a unique possibility: an opportunity to utilize your practical experience to bring a real-world understanding of the problems we address, and to assure our efforts are not simply good theory."

Sigsbee nodded.

"What I have conceived is to name you, Stu, as my 'Special Assistant'—in other words—as my troubleshooter. You will report directly to me and your job is to move freely about our councils, committees, and people to identify any problems of application you find and offer recommendations for rectifying the problem. Your Assistant—note I didn't say 'your Aide'—will undertake any assignments you believe will assist you and Tenth Fleet in the completion of our assigned responsibilities."

Sigsbee was thoughtful. Ed was skeptical.

"Comments, gentlemen? You first, Captain…"

Ed phrased his thoughts carefully:

"Admiral, please understand that this is a new world for me—so I am speaking from ignorance. Sir, it seems to me that an occasional lecture from the seagoing community would serve to inject some knowledge of the practical applications of the work here. I'm having trouble picturing what our actual actions would be on a daily basis. Again—I'm in a situation I'm unfamiliar with, so I hesitate to even comment…"

Low nodded: "Stu?"

"Well, it's pretty open-ended, but I know how effective a 'Special Assistant' can be. I think this might be a very effective way of assuring a dose of reality." He smiled: "Also, I am sure my 'Assistant' will quickly adjust to his new role—this man really knows how to lead, and how to inspire his followers. I think, together, we can make a genuine contribution."

"Good! So you—both—accept this new assignment?"

Palmer: "Yes, sir!"

Sigsbee: "Yes, sir!"

Admiral Low grinned:

"Excellent! Then let's move on to the more pragmatic details: We have located a suitable office for you—it's not palatial, but it's far from being a janitor's closet. It's right here on second deck and not too far from where we are right now. Next—wheels: I have ordered that car be assigned to you and it should be downstairs awaiting you. A question arises regarding a driver…"

Stu looked at Ed and smiled and Ed grinned back.

"Now what?"

"I'm sorry, Francis," Stu responded, "but Ed and I just had this discussion about drivers. The coincidence is amusing…"

"Oh. Well, at any rate, do you have any suggestions regarding a driver? We can certainly assign you one…"

Ed spoke:

"Gentlemen, despite my angst about becoming an 'Admiral's driver', it seems to me that, given our living situation, it makes sense for me to drive. I can keep the car where I'm staying, pick Stu up each morning, and drive us here. That's rather than having a driver who lives at the Navy Yard having to commute all the way out to Woodley Park and back every morning and evening."

Low nodded. Sigsbee smiled.

"OK, Captain, that seems a reasonable suggestion."

They continued their conversation detailing various other day-to-day matters and finally concluded a little after 15:15. Stu and Ed headed for their office—#2428.

Their office consisted of two well-dented metal desks and two well-dented metal four-drawer filing cabinets—double what they had before! Progress in Washington seemed to happen in small steps—but at least it was located within the Tenth Fleet area and it was close to the CNO's office. Stu just smiled wryly:

"Oh, well—we'll make it better…"

*   *   *   *   *   *   *

Later that evening during a brief period of quiet time, Ed was reflecting on recent events:

The last six months have been astounding—Woodside fought the U-boats and won. Now we're here in Washington and I'm commanding a desk…Grrr! The bureaucracy and ineptitude here make me wonder how we'll win the war. I sure don't want to join the "cocktail circuit"! There's a whole lot more war to go, and I want to be a part of it!

*   *   *   *   *   *   *

The first weeks of June had seen great upheaval in the lives of many people once associated with *USS Woodside.* It seemed the wolfpacks were subdued, but there was a lot more war to fight. Germany, Italy, and Japan were far from beaten, even though the United States had enjoyed some victories after the long string of earlier defeats. By mid-1943, the course of the war seemed to be pivoting for the Allies—but to prevail would require a full effort from every American. *Woodside,* Stu, Ed, Prof, and all the others would be called on to make unimaginable efforts to overcome the implacable and evil foes in order to return freedom and peace to the world. And therein lies a story…

THE END

I hope you enjoyed *Fangs of the Wolf*.

Book 4: *The Sun Sets Westward*

Should be available Fall, 2021.

Printed in Great Britain
by Amazon

17045263R00153